The Homesteaders

Also by Richard Clarke

The Copperdust Hills

The Homesteaders

Richard Clarke

Walker and Company
New York

First published in the United States of America
in 1986 by the Walker Publishing Company, Inc.

Published simultaneously in Canada by John Wiley & Sons
Canada, Limited, Rexdale, Ontario.

ISBN 0-8027-4054-5

Book Design by Teresa M. Carboni

Printed in the United States of America

10 9 8 7 6 5 4 3 2 1

Contents

870
8 - 1

CHAPTER 1

Peralta

PEOPLE called him Moneyman. He was a large, fleshy individual in his fifties who had at one time, before a sedentary existence had eliminated his need for exercise, been as strong as a bull.

His name was James McGregor. He was president of the Northern New Mexico Livestockmen's Savings Bank at Peralta, had come to New Mexico from Missouri thirty years earlier with a redheaded wife named Angela, and after her death devoted himself almost exclusively to the bank's affairs.

He had thinning gray hair, keen eyes the color of creek pebbles, a wide thin mouth, and the jaw of a person to whom compromise was probably more nearly a three-syllable word than a desirable course of action.

He had reorganized the bank after assuming the presidency upon the death of old John Alden White, its founder—and also the founder of the largest and richest cattle ranch in either Southern Colorado or Northern New Mexico.

And he had made the bank prosper, which its late founder had never quite been able to do. Not only prosper, but reach out for depositors for several hundred miles in all directions. Old John Alden White had been a cattleman; he had declined accounts which were not based on the livestock industry. James McGregor had mining accounts, freighting accounts, a host of small-venture accounts such as those of the Peralta Tanning & Harness Works, The Peralta General Store & Emporium, O'Bryon's Livery and Drayage Barn, and, in several distant towns, additional merchants' accounts.

He had not accomplished all this without being shrewd,

careful, and tough. To the remark people made about no one liking a banker, McGregor's answer was basically a reflection of his personal conviction: "Try making a country grow without one. The next time you need a loan try getting one from your neighbors."

Jim McGregor was a large piece of Peralta's bedrock. He had preferences exactly as old John Alden White had had, but McGregor's dedication to the bank was based entirely upon making the bank's money work. How much land or cattle someone had, or how thriving their stage, freight or mercantile business might be concerned him only to the extent that their deposits were healthy and they did not ask for loans.

He was not against loaning bank money but his responsibility was to make certain borrowers would not default and his policy in this regard was never to loan money to people who did not already have funds on deposit with the bank.

As Kelly O'Bryon of the Peralta Livery and Drayage Company at the lower end of town once said to Constable Cutler, "Newcomers can starve to death while the White family with their big cow outfit, and their likes, can get money any time they want it—because they don't need it."

Constable Cutler had sat in silence neither agreeing nor disagreeing. He worked for wages and lived within them. He maintained order, enjoyed faro, horse-racing, and although large and powerful and young, with a reputation for being able to clean out the saloon with just his hands, was an easygoing man. Some said he was lazy.

He and Kelly O'Bryon met every Thursday night at the Horseshoe card room, which was behind a red drapery separate from the saloon's bar, and played cards—faro, poker, Pedro, and occasionally twenty-one, also called blackjack. There were two other players in those sessions: Fred Tower, who operated the Peralta tannery, which had branched out a few years earlier to include a saddle and harness sideline, and Gus Heinz, a pale-eyed, bull-necked grizzled cowman who was built like one of those milestones at distant intervals on the north-south stageroad: They were blocks of pure granite, massive and shapeless, erected at considerable labor, and with considerable profanity, to replace the wooden mileage-markers which had preceded them and which irresponsible sons of guns used for target practice while leaning out of moving stagecoaches.

Gus, like Jim McGregor, was a widower. Unlike Jim he'd had children before his wife died. Two sons, also pale-eyed men, but taller and rangier than their compact father. They pretty well ran things, along with three hired riders. For seven miles the Heinz range bordered the White outfit. After fifteen years and a series of confrontations over straying cattle, among other things, there was a distinct coolness between the outfits.

As Gus said at one of the back room card games in early spring: When old John Alden had been alive there had been no trouble. He and Gus had an agreement; whoever had to drive back the other's livestock kept track of his time and took it out in whiskey in town, or, if it was needed, lent a hand at roundup time.

The stockmen had thought highly of John Alden White. Not everyone in town did, for various reasons, but now that he was inside the wrought-iron fence at the ranch graveyard, people were inclined to shrug and forget.

Fred Tower, who was a lanky tobacco-chewing man from Indian Territory, had disliked John Alden because he had opposed the establishing of a tannery in Peralta's town limits. Fred had gone ahead anyway and the two men never spoke again.

Shortly before John Alden died townspeople—who had disliked his high-handed opposition to Fred's tannery for their own private reasons, mostly based on envy of his wealth and social position—had to agree that he had been right, the tannery should never have been allowed in the center of town. Aside from the flies, tanning vats had an aroma that would gag a buzzard and, if the wind blew, the smell went all over town.

A couple of years after John Alden had been planted the Peralta town council yielded to the demands of the townsfolk and summoned Fred to a closed meeting, at which the chairman, Jim McGregor, told Fred he would have to move his vats out of town.

Fred had moved them. He was neither unreasonable nor antagonistic. He did possess a temper—he had once whipped a big burly freighter to a fare-thee-well in the center of the roadway—but ordinarily, lanky and graying Fred Tower was a shrewd, easygoing, friendly man. He had arrived in northern New Mexico driving a wagon for a Texas drover. At that time he'd owned a bedroll, two guns, an old battered A-fork Texas saddle, and the clothes he was standing in. Peralta had been good to him. Moving the vats was troublesome and expensive, but Fred never denied they drew flies and smelled bad. What he never mentioned was that he felt he owed something to the community; it had helped him prosper.

He was single, had never married, and probably would have made some woman a fine husband. He had that loyal, fair, and honest disposition, capped with a dry sense of humor, that made for a faithful provider. But it had just never happened and at fifty-odd the chances were that it never would.

He took some kidding about being single, and took it well, like the Thursday evening they were at their table behind the red velvet curtain with a springtime drizzle keeping folks indoors, and Walt Cutler, the town constable, mentioned something about those settlers who had homesteaded the broad neck of land among the scrub hills west of the White-ranch range. Someone down at the general store had told him the settler-lady was right handsome for being into her forties or thereabouts and her man wasn't much. "She'd most likely appreciate a helping hand," the constable said slyly without looking up from his cards.

Fred looked over, his expression bland. "Even a settler could shoot a trespasser," he said. "You got openers, Walt?"

"Nope. You, Gus?"

Heinz held his cards so close to his chest he had to rock his head back to see them. He had openers so the game began. While discarding, Gus winked at Walt Cutler and spoke to the cards he was holding. "They'll go belly-up. Settlers usually do.

This ain't plow land; it may look like it but it ain't . . . Do them a favor, Fred, ride out and tell 'em before they lose everythin' and starve out. The lady ought to be grateful."

Jim McGregor had nothing to add to this conversation; he played poker the same way he conducted the bank's affairs, to win. He was holding three of a kind and he was playing against three other men. Most players would have raised but McGregor didn't. He dropped out then waited to see if that had been a mistake. It hadn't been; Constable Cutler had a full house.

Walt raked in the pot and passed the deck to McGregor as he drifted away from the settler-woman but not the subject of settlers. "I know that neck of land. The Whites used it for calving out their first-time heifers. It's protected on three sides." He picked up his cards and studied them before saying anything more. It was a dead hand anyway; he kept the ace and discarded everything else.

"I think they could maybe raise potatoes and turnips and the like up there, Gus. It's deeper ground than out beyond."

Heinz closed his cards and held them close as he gazed across the table. "Maybe," he conceded, blue eyes on the lawman, their expression speculative and dispassionate. "If I was a settler the last place I'd homestead would be on land adjoinin' a cow outfit that'd always used that land."

The subject was allowed to die: Jim McGregor had a royal flush; the other players were very impressed. Filling a hand to that extent was something to think about. McGregor hauled in the pot and settled back, fishing for a cigar in a coat pocket, and because he was feeling very pleased and expansive now, he lit up, blew smoke, and said, "This isn't Wyoming, Gus. People don't sneak around in the night burning settlers out and shooting their livestock—especially the Whites; they own more land and have more money and cattle than you can shake a stick at."

Heinz squinted a little but said nothing. Not until he had lost the next hand and leaned to pick up his shot glass of whiskey. Then he eyed the banker a trifle caustically as he said, "Jim, we're on different sides of the fence about the Whites. Old John Alden was a friend of mine like he was a friend of yours. When he died things changed between me'n the Whites. You feel loyalty toward them. All I got is some nasty talk from their rangeboss about my cattle bein' on their range—and a few other things." Gus paused long enough to pick up the cards Fred Tower had dealt him and squint at them. Then he also said, "Like I said earlier—if I was a settler I wouldn't homestead no land an outfit like that's been using for first-calf heifers all these years."

McGregor played his hand and lost to Fred Tower; they all lost to Fred. McGregor settled ash from his stogie in a bowl and regarded the lighted tip for a moment while he considered his reply, but when he raised his eyes Walt Cutler was looking straight at him with no trace of a smile. Jim plugged the cigar between his teeth, clamped down on it, and concentrated on his cards.

An hour later while McGregor and Constable Cutler were standing beneath the overhang out front of the saloon, Jim said, "I lost two dollars, how about you?"

Walt was studying the wet overcast when he answered. "Lost half a dollar. Gus did pretty well tonight."

McGregor also leaned to squint upwards. Rain did not interest him the way it did rangemen. "Gus's got a hard disposition," he murmured. "The Whites wouldn't make trouble for a settler. They don't have to, Walt. They can sit back and wait, then pick up the pieces for a dime on the dollar."

Constable Cutler thought that was probably true but for some reason he did not like the way McGregor had said it—with contempt in his voice. "See you tomorrow," he said, smiled, and went hiking through the mud of the wide roadway to reach the far side before turning northward. The rooming house was on that side of the road. He'd had a room there for almost six years now. It wasn't much but on rainy nights like this one it beat hell out of having to live under a tree.

Peralta turned dark a little at a time. The last building to darken was the saloon. On Saturday nights it did business past midnight but that rarely happened during the week. The rain continued to fall, softly, gentle, and warm without force, exactly the kind of rainfall stockmen lay awake in their beds listening to as though it were music. Especially in the late springtime.

CHAPTER 2

The
Willow Spring

PERALTA had no doctor: It had a midwife and an old man named Bellingham who worked for Kelly O'Bryon and who had experience in treating animals, particularly horses and mules. Otherwise illnesses and broken bones in Peralta were "doctored" at home. Old Bellingham was especially good with broken bones. It was also claimed that he'd been a Confederate Army doctor and knew a lot about bullet wounds, but that was rumor and Bellingham himself, a stringbean of a man, weathered and bent, said nothing. He drank a lot and slept in the hay at O'Bryon's place, a solitary old man who rarely spoke.

The nearest medical doctor was down at Mineral Springs, which had a railroad siding with corrals and was the terminus for cattle drives from all directions. It was also twenty-two miles southeast of Peralta, and aside from the doctor's fee of three dollars on the barrelhead if he had to drive up as far as Peralta to treat someone, if bleeding was involved he probably would never arrive in time. It was a full day's drive by buggy from Mineral Springs to Peralta. And three dollars was a lot of money.

Among the settlers who had been arriving in the Peralta country over the last five or six years to "take up" land from the government and establish homesteads, three dollars was not exactly a fortune, it was simply something they almost never possessed, and it was known that the doctor from Mineral Springs would not accept garden vegetables, calves, puppies from good hunting dogs, or fowl—only cash money.

The settlers helped one another although at times that was a real hardship because there were not many of them and their homesteads were usually many miles apart. The Bartlett place, for example, was up a wide neck of land bordered by the White cattle outfit. To reach it from three directions visitors had to cross the White range and while it was common practice to cross the land of others in this huge, fenceless area, for settlers to do this had resulted in some hard words and fistfights. Settlers were not welcome additions to cattle country and not just in New Mexico.

A rider approaching the Bartlett homestead from Peralta, which was about seven miles southward, skirted White range but only actually crossed it for about a half mile. This was the route the Bartletts had used to locate their land, and afterwards to go down to Peralta for supplies. It was also the route Elizabeth Bartlett had used in her search for a doctor when her husband began to fail. She had found none in Peralta, but had been told of the medical man twenty-two miles southeast—and what he would charge to drive up and examine her man.

Elizabeth had fourteen red hens. After the visit to Peralta she began hoarding eggs to be sold in town. She had almost accumulated the full doctor's fee within two months when foraging coyotes had raided the yard killing ten of her red hens.

She walked out a mile to a little seepage spring where berry bushes grew amid a bosque of little willow trees, sat down, and cried.

Elizabeth was five and a half feet tall, lithe, supple, and strong. She wasn't in her forties as someone had said in town, she was thirty-five. But she had a tracing of silver at the temples which was especially noticeable because her hair was a very dark red-auburn color.

But the rest of the town judgment had been correct. She was a handsome woman with a full, determined mouth, gray-green eyes, and despite hardship and exposure, her skin was perfectly clear and the color of new cream.

She was work-hardened; her hands were large and blue-veined. She had been orphaned back in Missouri when a little short of her teens and had been put in a State workhouse. She had met Harry Bartlett during her eighteenth year. He had left Missouri the following year and did not return from the sea until Elizabeth was in her late twenties and was working as a seamstress in St Joseph. They were married, Harry's savings went for a road outfit, and they had "taken up" land sight unseen.

The overland crossing had been a mixture of hardship and a variety of happiness Elizabeth had not known was possible. It made the worst of the crossing bearable.

They had located their land, built a log house, a three-sided woodshed, and turned their chickens loose. Their insular happiness left no room for the ignorance each possessed in great abundance. Northern New Mexico was not Missouri. In Missouri it rained, in New Mexico their first-year oat crop headed out at six inches then shriveled like corn husks in the rainless summer.

One of their harness horses developed thrush during the second winter, and although they knew what to do and did it, the horse was unable to put his weight on that one hoof even after hot weather returned.

Harry began to tire easily during the autumn of the second year. Into the winter his summer cough worsened, he had very little appetite, drank a lot of water, and finally had periods of irrationality during which he ran a high fever and his face shone red beneath an unseasonal sweat.

Then the coyotes had come.

Elizabeth hugged her knees beside the little cold-water spring, gazing down where their log house and woodshed stood in golden sunlight. Almost all of their one hundred and sixty acres was in the wide swale of the "neck" between low hills which bristled with rotting tree stumps. Once the setting had been bordered by majestic firs and pines. Woodcutters had gleaned everything down to saplings. Throughout the West there were huge tracts of this cut-over land. It was considered useless. The government added it to the land open to settlers. The homesteads were called stump ranches.

But in Bartlett's valley the land was rich and deep, there was shelter on three sides from winter winds, and there was a creek near the yard. Elizabeth loved this hidden, private place with its shy deer, its multicolored wildflowers in springtime, its aura of peacefulness—and the love she and Henry shared in their isolated world which held it all together.

Henry was dying of lung fever. She had seen people die of it back in Missouri. She closed her eyes to blot out the lovely meadow, the pure sky, the wildflowers, the log buildings they had built together with laughter over their lack of carpentering skill, and the thin caricature of her stalwart man on the cot in the overheated combination parlour and kitchen down there where the four remaining red hens scratched for seeds and bugs.

Because Elizabeth had never known anything but hardship she accepted it as the normal price for survival. It was physical: it was drought, deluges, brush and timber fires, it was waterless days during a prairie crossing, it was lost time waiting for storms to pass while huddling in the cold of a wagon with a leaky canvas top. It was enduring the perversities of natural calamities which were never mild—but it was not a dying of the heart, a shriveling of the soul and spirit. It was not the totally descending night of absolute desolation.

She opened her eyes. Everything down there was the same except that she could no longer see the beauty nor even feel the love except in herself. Much of the time Henry did not know who she was.

She sat huddled and oddly detached remembering their plans, their dreams, their faith in the future. She would have been willing to die and even the sound of shod hooves coming down the eastern slope behind her belonged to the world she seemed to be withdrawing from, right up until a man's hard voice said, "Lady, that crippled horse of yours was over on White range. I brought him back, but next time maybe not."

The rider swung the turk's-head end of his lariat to strike her crippled horse across the rump and send it in a crablike run past her down toward the meadow.

She could feel the horse's pain as though the man had struck her with his lariat. She had never had such an experience before; it was actual physical pain. It brought her back to the world of a clear sky and sunshine very abruptly. She sprang up to turn with a heavy stone in her right fist, gray-green eyes blazing.

She knew him—not his name but that he was one of the White ranch rangeriders. He had sat on the rims many times, a motionless and menacing statue, looking down into their hidden meadow. He was a burly, unshaven, faded man with very dark eyes and a jaw which was much too massive for the upper part of his face. Henry had said he did that to intimidate them. If so, he had succeeded, at least with Elizabeth, but now all she saw was the brutish face, the bullying expression, and the gloved hands deliberately coiling the lariat without looking at her, his attitude one of absolute contempt.

She made an animal cry just before hurling the piece of gray granite with all her strength. At the sound the man turned his head. For two seconds his eyes widened, then the rock struck him squarely between the eyes.

The horse shied, the thickly built man fell without making any attempt to break the fall, and the horse moved clear before looking dumbly back. Then it dropped its head and began cropping grass.

For a full minute Elizabeth's breath came and went in deep sweeps as though she had been running. It required that much time for the full force of the previous moment to hit her. It had happened too suddenly. The entire interlude had lasted no more than ten seconds. She was not even conscious now of hurling the piece of granite. She simply knew that something wild had broken loose inside, a blind and savage—and sound-less—scream of black despair and mind-stunning physical pain.

The soft music of rein-chains and the distant high-strident cry of a circling red-tailed hawk brushed across her awareness with total clarity. She moved her eyes from the face-down rangeman to look at the horse, then to twist in the direction of the log buildings in their peaceful setting a mile away in the clear distance.

Her knees were weakening as she faced forward so she sank down into the grass, and finally began willing the man to move, to lift his head, even to glare at her with raw hatred and fury.

He lay motionless.

The sun had noticeably shifted down the flawless sky before Elizabeth arose, unconsciously brushed grass off her skirt, and stepped over close enough to see rusty congealing blood on two sides of the rangeman's head where it had trickled from both ears. It was no longer trickling; it was drying dark in the grass. His forehead too was bloody.

By firmly blocking out what instinct told her about this rangeman she spoke to him, reached to shake him gently by the shoulder, and finally sat down beside him, forming with her lips words that had no sound.

He was dead. She touched him again, then drew back staring, because it was just simply impossible. He was a thickly muscular individual: If she could have thought of one word to describe him it would have been—durable.

He had flecks of gray in the shaggy hair over his ears. He looked asleep. There had been no gush of blood, no outpouring, and his clothing had no blood on it. He was still wearing the shiny old buckskin roping gloves, his fingers softly curled in the rank grass.

She studied the gun in its hip-holster and the gaps in his belt where there were no handgun casings. His spurs were silver overlaid on the outside, his boots were badly worn, his trousers, like his old butternut shirt, were old and faded. He should have gotten up and gone to catch his horse.

It was an effort for her to arise, facing down the slope in the direction of the log house where the mellow glow approaching sundown softened rough corners.

Henry. She had been gone too long. He would be needing drinking water and maybe he would take some broth. He would need to be washed and helped to the outhouse. She had been gone too long, so she picked her way downhill from the little spring in its setting of willows and berry bushes, increasing her pace as anxiety increased her need to reach her husband in the safety of their little log house.

She was almost running by the time she reached flat ground. There were shadows on the lee side of the meadow up along the south sidehill where raw, rotting old stumps thrust up several feet out of the undergrowth and hummocks of buffalo grass.

Up on the east slope the saddled horse watched her grow small, and in a dim part of his brain knew that this day was ending. He eyed the dead man, and when the man did not move, the horse turned back up the slope carrying his head slightly to one side so as not to step on the reins and followed his homing instinct.

CHAPTER 3

After Nightfall

THE cabin was hot and seemed hotter to Elizabeth because of her exertion from running, but her husband was shivering upon the edge of the cot with an old blanket around his shoulders, his face sweat-wet and feverishly red. His eyes followed her from the door to the stove, their brightness missing no detail as he gathered the blanket closer.

She fed wood into the stove and straightened up to pat her hair and control her breathing before she turned and smiled as she said, "I'll heat the broth," then used the dipper to scoop spring water from the bucket and take it to him. He drank greedily then gathered the blanket closer to his emaciated body.

The cold water seemed to briefly amelioriate the fever, as had happened before. He said, "Liz . . . I love you."

The same lump closed her throat as at other times when he had been lucid. She locked her jaws against the same urge to cry at the desperate look in his eyes, his expression of dread and loss. His features blurred as she placed a cool palm against his face and said, "I love you, Henry. I always will love you."

He clutched the blanket closer and shivered. His eyes moved around the room from the table and chairs they had made to the iron stove they had hauled from Peralta in the wagon when both team horses had been sound, and came back to Elizabeth. What she read in the depths of his eyes was not despair. It was the knowledge of a terrible certainty. In a perfectly rational tone of voice he said, "I don't know . . . What will happen to you, Liz? Oh God I don't want this to happen! I prayed —prayed. God, Elizabeth . . ."

She knelt and used up nearly all her remaining strength to

smile into his eyes. "Nothing will happen to me. You know how tough I am . . . I'm going down to Peralta and send for that doctor from Mineral Wells." At his stare, she lied to him. "We have the money." She gripped his wasted big hands in both her hands, forcing the smile to be encouraging though the pain in her heart was almost unbearable and the mist in her eyes had increased.

Because she was losing her battle for control she abruptly arose and turned toward the stove as she said, "I'll heat the broth. Do you want me to help you to the outhouse?"

The answer behind her was quietly said. "No, Liz, I don't think you should spend the money for that doctor. I think you should keep it for later. I think the sound horse is worth maybe fifteen dollars, and the claim . . ."

She got very busy at the stove because she could not face him. "We'll need the horse to fallow the land come autumn, and the claim—is our special place, Henry." She felt heat from the stove rising to stifling temperatures; he was always cold even when it was insufferable in the cabin. She mopped sweat off her face and put the blue-ware pot on a burner. "We need the doctor, Henry, otherwise you'll most likely be a long time getting your strength back."

He looked at her from eyes which had lost their brilliance. At first when he had begun to tire easily and the cough had doubled him over, they had blamed it on dust and perhaps overwork. Then they pretended there was no cough, no tiredness, no diminishing appetite. When late spring had brought pollen from the sidehills, ragweed, sage, lupin and goldenrod, they had seized upon that too, and after the time of pollen had passed they stopped talking about his illness as though by blinding themselves to it, refusing to recognize its existence, they could will it away.

They hadn't been able to.

He said, "The Mortons, Liz . . . I wish the Mortons would drive over."

She was testing the broth and that delayed her response. The Mortons lived eleven miles away—about thirty miles if to reach the Bartlett place they had to skirt around White Ranch range. The broth was hot, so she filled a cup and with a spoon in hand finally turned, her face as red as his, but for a different reason, and she pushed up the smile again while approaching the bed.

His appetite had left. In its place was an almost dumb-brute fatalism that looked out of his eyes at her. She could feel the strength ebbing from him as certainly as she had felt the physical pain when that man had struck their crippled horse. It took her to her knees beside him, robbing her of all strength and will.

She cried in his lap as the shadows lengthened out across their meadowland.

By early dusk she had eased him flat down and had mounded the blankets over his shivering frame. The feverish brightness of his eyes told her irrationality had returned.

Her body seemed very heavy as she willed herself to cross to the door and open it to let cool fresh air inside. She leaned for support on rough wood—and saw movement a mile away up the easterly sidehill.

Three horsemen were up there on foot near the willow-spring, holding reins as they shifted slightly, turning a little toward something which seemed to be holding their attention. Even at that distance in the failing daylight she could sense their shock.

While she knew what they were staring at, she had been too emotionally drained over the last couple of hours to do more than just lean in the doorway looking up there. The fear did not arrive then, or the horror.

The horsemen stood talking and one twisted westward to motion toward the log house. The others also turned, standing like stone for a long while until someone made a matter-of-fact remark. Then all three of them leaned to hoist the corpse and push it belly-down across someone's saddle and tie it.

The man whose horse was burdened with the corpse led his animal up the westerly slope behind his companions who were astride, and did not mount behind the cantle until they were on the skyline.

She saw them as shadowy shapes in the deepening dusk as they sat there gazing back down toward the log house for a few moments before turning and disappearing down the far side of the hill.

Then the horror and fear arrived.

It had not occurred to her to hide the corpse. Nor had it occurred to her that they could have backtracked the riderless horse so quickly. Just then it did not register with her that the people of the man she killed had coveted this protected neck of land, and so had been hostile to Elizabeth and her husband for three years now, and had all the reason people ever needed in cattle country to return.

She closed the door, lighted two candles, sat at the table looking at her fitfully sleeping husband, and clasped both hands in a mood of numb lassitude, and after a while lowered her head to her folded arms and slept.

She did not hear the wolves running out beyond the wide opening of their meadow, which faced westward, and she did not feel the creeping cold which came inside long after the fire-box of the stove held nothing but light gray ash.

She had not thought beyond her horror. That, more than the fear of what would happen now as a result of her having killed a man, had completed for Elizabeth what the emotional draining had begun when she had returned to the cabin to find Henry waiting and rational.

She had reached beyond the point of feeling anything, which was when the overpowering need to close her eyes had come.

It was a long night with a sickle-moon and was leavened by a faint fragrance of wildflowers. A high rash of stars made a pewter ribbon of the stageroad which ran arrow-straight down into Peralta.

There were three visible lights on Main Street. One was at the Horseshoe Saloon, another was down in front of O'Bryon's barn, and the third light showed through the two little recessed barred front windows at the Peralta jailhouse where Walt Cutler was performing his final chore of the day: making an entry in the jail log. He'd locked up a traveling peddler who had got drunk at the Horseshoe and refused to leave when asked to.

In the morning he would herd the prisoner up to the office, pour black java into him, read off the statute which permitted the town-constable to levy a five-dollar fine, and see that he left the town.

Walt was tired. He'd had a full day, and when he slapped the log book closed and reached for his hat a whisper of faint sound kept him motionless until it became loud enough to be identified: Horsemen coming into town from the north.

He arose, dumped the hat on the back of his head, and crossed to the door.

There were three of them, or perhaps four. They were just reaching the north end of town and with visibility not very good he was un-sure, so he stepped outside, closed the door at his back, and leaned in overhang-darkness to wait.

They rode slowly, which prolonged his wait. Until they were passing the harness works, which was opposite the saloon, he could not see any of them very well. They were another hundred or so feet southward riding in a bunch before he made out that there was a led horse with a dead man tied across it.

Walt's tiredness vanished.

When they were veering toward his little lighted windows he recognized the foremost rider as Mack Kelso, White-ranch foreman, a tall, spare, taciturn individual for whom Walt Cutler had never felt any degree of warmth.

They saw Cutler move out of his shadows but dismounted to tie up without saying a word. They remained silent as Walt went over to raise the dead man's head, look at his face, then step away as he turned to say, "One of yours, Mack?"

Kelso nodded, drawing off his gloves and looking at his hands as he did this. "Yeah. His name was Ron Sexton." While folding the gloves under his gunbelt Mack raised his eyes. "Them settlers in the neck killed him."

Walt stepped back onto the boardwalk before saying, "How?"

The White-ranch rangeboss hung fire over his reply, perhaps

because the way Sexton had died bothered him. "Hit between the eyes with a rock."

He saw Walt Cutler's eyes widen. "With a rock, Mack?"

"Yeah. The front of his skull's got a hole in it. We got a piece of granite—Sam, fish that thing out." A smaller, wiry man dug in one saddlebag and handed the stone to Kelso, who held it out for Constable Cutler to take, which he did, and turned it in his fingers in the weak light. Then Cutler raised his face, wearing a faint scowl of doubt as he said, "Was he armed, Mack?"

"Yeah, he was armed," the rangeboss stated, getting more uncomfortable by the minute. "The horse come into the yard with his outfit on it and we backtracked it and found him. He was on his face near a little spring on that east sidehill about a mile up from the Bartlett shack."

Walt stared at the rock in his hand. He was beginning to sound puzzled when he said, "Well, this cowboy—what was he doing over there?"

Mack Kelso could give a valid reply to this question because he was good at reading signs. "Those settlers got two harness horses. One of 'em is crippled. He was leading a crippled horse toward their homestead. It was too dark to make out much by the time we found Ron by the willow-spring, but sure as hell he'd found their horse where it had no right to be, on our range, and taken it back . . . Beyond that all I know is that somehow they hit him with that rock and busted his skull."

Mack Kelso shifted stance and looked once at the two rangemen who had accompanied him to town with the corpse, then settled his dark gaze on the big constable again. Walt was faintly scowling at him and that annoyed him too so he said, "I don't know how they did it, Walt. In'ians killed folks that way, and settlers—well—maybe Bartlett used a slingshot. I wouldn't put anythin' past those sons of guns. They let their horses graze over onto us and have for a year or so; don't make any effort not to. That's how settlers work, Walt, take an inch, a foot, a yard, and if they aren't stopped . . ." Kelso considered the corpse and spoke aside to his riders. "Take him down . . . Walt, you got a place in your back room . . . ?"

Walt led the way, stood aside while Ron Sexton was placed on the floor, then went after a cell-room blanket so they could cover him. As he was closing the door after them he said, "Mack, maybe the horse bucked him off in the rocks and—"

"That horse never bucked in his life," the rangeboss stated emphatically. "An' if he had Ron could have rode him out." He nodded toward the rock as Constable Cutler placed it atop his desk. "A man don't bust his skull going off a horse and hitting something like that, Constable. It might cut his hide and give him a headache—if he didn't fling up his arms to protect his face—but fallin' on that thing wouldn't have busted his skull. That rock hit him goin' fast. I can tell you that Bartlett feller is strong enough to throw a rock that hard."

Walt sighed and went to his chair. "Have you folks and those people been jangling a little?"

Kelso's very dark eyes were level and uncompromising. "No. We stayed away from over there. My orders was to leave those people strictly alone. I passed that along to the riders. But we had call to . . . him lettin' his horses trespass and all. Only we didn't."

"Then what was Sexton doing over there?"

"I already told you; he'd found one of their horses on our range and taken it back. That's all. Ron worked for us—this is his first season but I knew him better'n I know you. If anythin' he was doing them a neighborly favor. He wasn't lookin' for trouble. And he sure as heck wasn't expecting any. The tie-down's still on his gun. That guy sure enough waylaid him somehow and maybe used a slingshot to kill him with that rock."

The conversation had gone nowhere and was now beginning to travel in circles so Walt Cutler arose from his chair as he said, "All right. Stay away from the neck, Mack. I'll go out there tomorrow. What about the body? There's a graveyard at the ranch."

Kelso was pulling on his gloves as he replied. "Yeah, we'll bring in a wagon for it. I wanted you to see it exactly as we found it." He finished with the gloves while looking steadily at the constable. "The boss is in Omaha and won't be back for a couple of weeks. He's not goin' to like this."

Walt did not like it either; what he particularly did not like was the bizarre way the cowboy had been killed. He was not satisfied in his mind that Sexton had been downed with the rock on his desk. But one point Mack Kelso had made was a plumb fact: settlers were different. He had known Bartlett, at least to nod to in town, and had never seen the man wearing a gun. But for that matter he'd never seen him with a slingshot either.

He shook his head. "A slingshot, for Chrissake?"

After the White-ranch riders had departed Walt took a lamp into the storeroom and examined the corpse. The skull had indeed been hit but because of caked blood and the swelling it was impossible to see more. Squarely between the eyes and about two inches higher.

When he'd been a kid he'd killed rabbits with a slingshot and had in fact become a dead shot with one of the things, so as he knelt there looking at the gray face with flakes of dried blood in the ears and down the neck, he could believe at close range someone experienced with a slingshot could have done this.

He returned to the office, blew out the lamp, and headed for the door shaking his head. Outside, the moon was lower, there was a chill to the night, and on his hike up to the rooming house he blew out a big sigh. He had been town constable at Peralta four years; before that he'd been a deputy sheriff two years in Idaho. He'd seen his share of dead man and never before one who had been killed by a stone.

CHAPTER 4

"It's Impossible!"

HE left the stageroad a few miles north of Peralta on an angling course over White-ranch range aiming toward the Bartlett place and had covered about another mile before he saw a rider traveling in the opposite direction, moving through sidehill shadows the early morning sunlight had not as yet burned away.

He faded from view behind a thicket of scrub pine and watched the distant rider. It was not too early for rangemen to be abroad, but that certainly did not look like a rangerider, although as far as he knew no one else was likely to be over here. If it was a rangerider it would have to be someone from the White outfit, and he had told White's rangeboss last night to stay away from the neck.

He had not been up here in a year or more, had had no call to, and he did not like being up here now. Ordinarily the Peralta countryside was quiet. In fact, excluding rowdy cowboys in town now and then, there had not even been a horse theft in Cutler's bailiwick for something like two years and Walt liked it that way.

Finally, the distant rider left those sidehill shadows and emerged into sunlight. At the same time he began angling southeasterly. He would pass less than a half mile from the scrub pines where Walt was patiently watching him.

Hell. It wasn't a man it was a woman, and it wasn't a stock horse it was a twelve-hundred pudding-footed harness horse. He did not know the Bartlett woman and not to his recollection had he ever seen her in town, but to his knowledge no one else lived up in this area. He thought about remaining where he was; she was heading toward town, which probably meant she was going after supplies. Where sunlight reached it made a color close to red-gold in her hair. She sat straight up on the oversize horse and looked neither left nor right. Even from a distance Walt's impression was of someone engrossed in thought.

He let her pass, remained among the scrub pines until she was a fair distance down-country, then struck out again, heading toward the low hillock which separated the neck from the southward country.

There was a pair of overgrown ruts angling around the base of the hill. He watched the ground for barefoot horse tracks, but evidently the woman had not used the road. She must have gone directly over the top of the hill, which would be the shortest way.

There were meadowlarks in the curing tall grass. The land seemed to get better the closer he got to the wide opening leading up into the neck. After so long a time with no cattle down here, the feed brushed his stirrups. He came around the hillock and could see up the wide meadow to the easternmost hill a mile or more west, which closed the neck off in that direction, and there was another hillock to the north to protect this place on that side too.

It was not hard to imagine the Whites' calving out heifers in this protected place. And as he settled for the last leg of his journey with the log house and a solitary outbuilding up ahead, he was satisfied with what he had said at the poker session last Thursday: This was deeper and richer earth than the rangeland beyond. It was a pity these homesteaders didn't have a few heads of livestock to keep the feed down.

He finally saw crushed grass where the woman had gone almost due southward; she had indeed taken the shortest route, up and over that south-side hill.

He was two-thirds up the neck in the direction of the log house wondering mildly why Bartlett didn't at least plant some parsnips, maybe some potatoes and squash—something any-way, to carry him through the winter the way other settlers did—when light reflecting off metal a mile or so westward up where some willow trees grew, caught and held his attention as he got closer to the log house.

Mack Kelso had mentioned finding his dead rider near a little spring on the eastern sidehill about a mile from the log house. Mack had been over this country before and knew about where that spring was Kelso had mentioned. It was just about where those willows stood, or about where he'd caught the momentary brilliance of sunlight bouncing off metal.

He rode toward the woodshed, which was to one side of the house, northward. His intention was to tie his horse in there out of direct sunlight. As he rode he squinted hard in case there was another flash of reflected light—but there wasn't.

He swung off and led his horse into the shed, which had been built to accommodate at least four cords of firewood, about what it took to get through a winter in northern New Mexico, but which now held less than a half cord. There was plenty of room. He loosened the latigo and left the horse looking around at its strange shelter.

He approached the house from around in front, stepped up onto the meager slab-wood porch, and raised a gloved fist to the door. He knocked three times, then listened for sounds of movement. There were none. He rattled the door the last time he knocked, then swore under his breath because it seemed he had ridden a long distance for nothing. He knew the woman was not here and evidently neither was the settler-man.

He turned down off the little porch, tugged unconsciously at his gloves while gazing around, then started down the north side of the horse to look out back. He had been unable to see all the area behind the house as he had been riding toward the front of it. He did not want to ride all the way back to town until he'd made certain the man was not around.

As he was clearing the side of the house it occurred to him that Bartlett had fled. If he had, it would be hard to believe he had not done so because he was a murderer.

Rounding the corner of the house close to the log wall Walt could see in all directions and there was no sign of anyone out there. One large old horse in hobbles, who seemed to be having an unusually hard time managing the things as he grazed along, was the only living, moving creature in sight.

Walt took a few steps to get closer to the back entrance of the house, where there was the customary white metal washbasin, pitcher, old feed sack roller towel, and a tin dish holding a chunk of brown soap. He did not expect to see the settler out there, not after his loud knocking around front, but he was moving in that direction anyway when the shock of being struck by a bullet took his breath away half a second before he heard the distant flat sound of the carbine.

He went down struggling to catch his breath, too stunned to react by rolling toward shelter, and although he felt no pain, his body would not respond properly when instinct told him to move and to keep moving until he reached the woodshed.

He knew where the shot had come from—up that distant easterly slope where he had seen the reflection and—dammit —that's what the reflection had been: sunlight bouncing off a gun barrel which was being raised to someone's shoulder when they had seen him down by the house.

He was holding himself together expecting the next shot as he forced his shocked body to move, to scramble and roll and claw dirt in the direction of the woodshed.

But there was no second shot and if there had been Cutler would not have heard it because he did not reach the woodshed. He was struggling to with every remaining ounce of willpower when something that felt like warm oily dark water began flowing upwards from the vicinity of his belt buckle. When it reached higher than his throat he simply stretched out in the dirt and flattened there without moving, loose as a rag.

Flies arrived, drawn by blood. The tied horse stamped when they buzzed around his legs. He turned to look at the prone figure where the flies were thicker. Later, with the sun off-center and beginning to acquire its afternoon hue of softly glowing rust, the horse shifted impatiently; it was both hungry and thirsty. It nickered a couple of times at the man, then gave that up as wasted effort and cribbed on the upright post it was tied to.

A faint noise from within the house brought its head around, ears alert, dark eyes watching the back of the house, but that hope too came to nothing so it went back to gnawing on the post.

Not until it heard another horse in the middle distance, out of its sight but approaching from the south somewhere, over near that round, thick, low hillock, did it nicker again, this time making a louder noise.

Then it waited, head turned as far as the reins would permit. When the rider came around the house the horse whinnied and stamped until dust flew, scattering flies in all directions.

The rider stopped dead-still and remained motionless for a long moment, then cried out, flung off the big pudding-footed animal and ran blindly to the prone man and dropped to both knees. For five or six seconds she hung there, staring. It was not Henry.

She pushed the inert body, saw the badge, and rolled Cutler onto his back. Then both hands flew to her mouth. There was blood everywhere, on the lawman's clothing, in the grass, drying darkly against the ground.

There was one thing Elizabeth had always responded to swiftly: human injury, the sight of blood or broken bones. She raised a hand to push away a heavy coil of coppery hair, then made her examination. She knew the man was alive because blood was still sluggishly leaking from his body. She sat back with thoughts like butterflies making erratic patterns in her mind, then she sprang up, got the basin and pitcher, returned with them and systematically pulled the torn clothing away and went to work sluicing the man's body in her search for the wound.

There were two wounds, one where the bullet had entered, another where it had exited, and although she had never seen a bullet wound before, she knew she was looking at one now as she gingerly sponged the wound in front.

She ran to the house for bandaging cloth, shot Henry a swift, helpless look, and ran back to the man in front of the woodshed. He was large and hard to move. Nor did it help that his dead weight was like a soggy sack of grain when she tried to balance him on his side in order to get at the second, larger and ragged, hole in back. He tended to flop back down so she ended up placing one knee as a prop to hold him in place.

It was hard and awkward but she did not stop trying. When she had him cleaned and bandaged and eased him onto his back again, her whole body was wringing wet, her hands shook, and as she dippered water to rinse them of the blood, she felt sick.

The horse was shifting, moving, rubbing against the pole, looking at her and occasionally nickering. She knew what it wanted and let it wait. She had to think of some way to get the man off the ground and inside the house. He was even heavier than her husband had been when he had been healthy.

There was no way she could move the man. For the time being there was nothing more she could do so she went after the tethered horse, took hobbles from behind the cantle, dumped the saddle and blanket, led the horse out by the reins, hobbled it, removed the bridle and watched it hop hungrily toward the grass. She also cared for the pudding-footed harness-horse. He hopped after the lighter animal with no interest in the two-legged things but a great amount of curiosity about the strange gelding.

She went to the house, worried about her husband, who was asleep. He had awakened though during her long absence, had used the commode pot, and had sank feebly back down on the bed afterwards. She covered him, fired up the stove, put the blue-ware pot on a burner, and went over to sit on the edge of the bed looking down at his sweaty, unshaven, shrunken face. She was exhausted. She was also unable to put thoughts into orderly sequence except for one: She needed her husband more than she had ever needed him before. Not just because of the unconscious man in front of the woodshed but because when she had paid the stage driver to deliver her written message to the doctor down at Mineral Wells she had heard a pair of yardmen discussing the killing which someone over at the café had mentioned as having happened out on the White ranch somewhere.

She did the only thing for the man in the yard she could think of doing: She took three old blankets out there, got one under him, between his back and the ground, and wrapped him in the other two. Later, she took broth out to him, but although she could spoon it into his mouth, he did not swallow until she massaged his throat—and then he choked. So she left him to feed Henry.

She had slightly better luck with her husband. He swallowed broth and drank a lot of water, but his gaze passed through her without any recognition at all and he was breathing faster and more shallowly than he had before she had left this morning. She washed his face with cool water, got him settled, and started to stand up. Her legs failed so she reached for a chair back and clung to it, taking down big, deep breaths of air. Whether this helped, or the abrupt weakness passed of its own accord, she remained beside the chair for a long time, until the blue-ware pot began to smoke. Then she removed it from the burner, half closed the stove damper, and got a cup of very hot broth for herself and sank down at the table to drink it.

Horses squealing brought her upright with a pounding heart, but it was not a posse, it was the lawman's saddle animal showing irritation at the big work horse who was trying so hard to be friendly he was being obnoxious.

The broth worked wonders. She went back into the yard with dusk coming and her mind perfectly clear. She sank to her haunches beside the wounded lawman and got a shock. His eyes were fixed on her with a steady, rational gaze. She put the back of one hand against his cheek as she had been doing with her husband for a year now in order to gauge the extent of his fever. Surprisingly he had none.

The man took several shallow breaths, then spoke in a thick tone of voice. "Who are you?"

She explained without mentioning her name. He continued to look upwards. He took more little breaths and spoke again.

"Bartlett?"

"Yes. Elizabeth Bartlett. Are you the constable from Peralta?"

"Yes . . ."

"I—thought I recognized you, from town." Her hands lay like dead doves against the rumpled dark cloth of a long, full skirt. She stared at him, feeling the tiredness which his eyes only partly showed. "Where is—your husband, Missus Bartlett?"

"In the house."

"How bad am I hurt . . . ?"

She made a small gesture in the direction of the bandaging. "You were shot. I don't know anything about such wounds, but the bullet must have struck you on a glancing angle—maybe you were moving when it hit. I think it struck your hipbone and instead of going through, went around and came out a little lower down. I don't know if any bones are broken but I don't think so. You lost a lot of blood, Constable. You must have been lying here most of the day. I don't understand why you are still alive."

His eyes never left her face. When she became silent he breathed a little more deeply and spoke again in the same thick voice. "It was morning. I saw you riding toward town. I rode in here . . . he was back yonder up the slope. He shouldn't have come back to the house . . . he should have headed out of the country."

Her eyes widened slowly. "Who—my husband? Do you believe Henry shot you?"

Cutler made no effort to reply. He had been struggling not to close his eyes during their talk and now the effort was becoming almost overpowering.

She spoke to him in a sharp, penetrating voice. "Henry didn't shoot you. He couldn't have. It's impossible."

Walt closed his eyes with her last two words barely penetrating his mind.

CHAPTER 5

Time's Passing

FOR Elizabeth the next day was the longest of her life. Henry was burning up. He gulped water exactly as a wounded animal would have, by pure instinct. The pupils of his eyes were enormous and very dark. She bathed him hoping to bring down the fever. His body was hot to the touch. Over the past few months he'd had periods of lucidity. Today he was illucid and inert, his breathing rasped and bubbled, and he seemed too feeble to respond when she moved him in the bed.

He did not eat, but each time she brought the dipper he greedily emptied it, then fell back.

The man out by the woodshed was in pain, and when she uncovered his wounds to cleanse and re-dress them, the flesh was splotchy purple, terribly swollen and hot. He did not look at her as she knelt at his side. There was sweat on his face long before the new day had any warmth in it.

She looked for signs of infection but was unable to determine whether there were any because of the discoloration and swelling.

She sat back studying the swollen little puckery bullet holes, and when she finally sought his eyes, he met her gaze and spoke hoarsely to her. "He was up—by that spring—on the east sidehill."

She twisted to look eastward. She did not think about his bushwhacker, she thought of the dead man, saw him as clearly in her mind as though she were still regarding him from a distance of two feet in stunned disbelief.

He spoke again. "You got any laudanum?"

She had no laudanum or anything else, such as whiskey,

which might have lessened his pain. "No . . . nothing." She studied the strong bones of his face, the even features and the faint shadow of beard stubble. "I'll get you something to eat."

He was looking straight up now, jaws locked. "Town," he muttered. She could not get him to Peralta even if she'd had the strength to lift him to the wagon-bed. There was a tongue on the wagon, they did not own shafts, and with only one horse capable of pulling the wagon it could not be done.

She stood up with new-day sunlight beginning to pour down into the meadow from the eastward hilltop. The horses were grazing a half mile out, and evidently the irritation which had made Constable Cutler's animals so disagreeable the day before had passed because all three animals were grazing companionably close to one another.

Otherwise the hills were still slightly shadowed and there was no movement or sound. Elizabeth breathed deeply of pure cool air and turned to look down again. The constable was watching her, his jaw loosened. Evidently the pain had diminished a little. She said, "I sent for the doctor. I told the man at the stage company corral yard how to find the meadow."

Cutler did not take his eyes off her and remained silent until she began to turn toward the house, then said, "Lady, I'm not hungry."

She nodded; she knew about men with fever. "If the doctor doesn't get here today I have to figure out a way to get you to Peralta. You can't lie out here on the ground, you'll get chilled."

His stare was direct and unblinking. He seemed to be trying to fathom something. She smiled slightly. "I'll make a texas over you to keep the sun off. We have some old wagon canvas."

He did not speak nor did he take his eyes off her. Something was troubling him. She did not ask what it was; she had more than enough worries of her own, did not need to borrow anyone else's.

He finally asked about his wound. She told him all she knew. "It is badly swollen. Your hip is as big as a flour sack and it's purple. There is fever too, but it doesn't look infected. That's what we have to worry about; it's healing, the holes are closing. It's not bleeding anymore. I think it will heal in time and the swelling will go down. You lost a lot of blood, Constable. I'm surprised you can even talk. But it's infection we have to worry about; that, and getting you in the house and off the ground. But I'm afraid to move you. Even if I could."

He glanced toward the house, which she interpreted to mean she could get help over there. She shook her head slightly, then walked into the shed for an armload of wood and passed him again on her way to the house.

Whatever she had put into the water she'd washed him with smelled like carbolic acid. It seemed to discourage the flies, and for all he knew it was helping the healing process. One thing he had learned was not to move, not so much as a toe. The pain came immediately if he even took a deep breath. As long as he was motionless it remained in abeyance. But his whole body ached as though he'd been doing hard manual labor. The ache he had no trouble accepting. It was no worse than other aches he'd had.

He was ill and drowsy, but sleep was a fitful rather than deep and satisfying experience. When the handsome woman returned and with systematic efficiency rigged up a canvas cover above him, he watched everything she did while wondering why her husband did not lend a hand. His conclusion was that he had indeed fled after the bushwhacking.

By early afternoon when she brought him water he detected tiredness—and something else—in her. But she was not talkative. She was solicitous about him but seemed detached. He attributed that to the loyalty she felt for her husband, the man Walt Cutler had become convinced was the bushwhacker who had tried to kill him.

She returned in late afternoon to feed him, and although he was thirsty, seemed always to be thirsty, he still had no appetite. Also, he was afraid to move, even to raise his head, because of the immediate flood of pain this caused, which was not confined to his wounds but went through his entire body.

This time, however, Elizabeth Bartlett fed him. She leaned

over so he would not have to lift his head. When he barely chewed she scolded him in a matter-of-fact manner, still impersonal, but unrelenting. When he had eaten all the food she had brought and she sat back regarding him, he said, "Lady, I don't think you'd let me die even if I wanted to."

Her answer was short. "Unless there's infection you're not going to die. I'll be back when it's cooler to change the bandage."

He watched her disappear through the rear door of the log house, and moving just his eyes, gazed at the shimmering faint streamer of wood-smoke arising from the stovepipe, wondering why she'd had that fire burning all day when it was at least a hundred degrees outside.

He moved his head an inch at a time until he could see eastward a mile or so up where willow trees and a flourishing berry thicket were. He could make out individual details of that place. That son of a gun had been a good shot to hit something the size of a man from that distance.

He turned back very slowly until he could study the rear of the log house. He suspected his bushwhacker was inside. There was nothing to indicate this was true except that the woman's voice reached over to where Walt was lying from time to time. The words were indistinguishable but the sound was audible. She would not be talking to herself.

He wondered what she had done with his gun and shellbelt. Not that it was going to matter for a long while. If he could not move or sit up, let alone stand up and walk, he was not going to be able to look in the house and, if her husband was in there, arrest him.

By early dusk, when she appeared with a big old dented washpan and some clean feed-sack towels, he was feeling much better—still weak as a kitten and unable to move without excruciating pain, but rational and less feverish. He watched her hunker down and peel back her sleeves without looking at him, and inwardly flinched from the pain he knew would come the moment she started bathing him.

She had been profiled to him. When she turned to face him he was shocked at the change in her face. There were dark shadows beneath her eyes, her cheeks looked sunken, her mouth was slack and lifeless, and the dullness of her eyes did not quite conceal moving shadows of anguish in their depths.

Then she went to work without a word, and although she was gentle she was also detached, and maybe that made her more efficient but it also made her seem lifeless to Walt Cutler.

She paused when the bandage had been removed to sit back studying the wounds. She remained like that so long Cutler's heart sank. "Infection?" he murmured.

She seemed jarred out of a reverie by his voice, shot him a fleeting look, then leaned forward with a wet cloth to begin sponging the hot flesh as she said, "I don't think so, Constable. The reason is because the fever is only around the wounds, otherwise the discolored and swollen flesh is cool to the touch . . . I'm not sure but I don't think there's infection . . . I hope the doctor gets here tomorrow."

He gritted his teeth when the pain started. Neither one of them said a word even after she had finished and was drying her hands, and Walt was relaxing a little at a time, being especially careful to lie absolutely still. She sat back, let her shoulders sag, and raised her face in the direction of the cabin. Her profile held Cutler's attention because of its indefinable depth of private, very personal, anguish.

She pushed upright to her feet, holding the wet rags and the basin, turned her face to him, and did not utter a sound. Then she went back to the house leaving Walt lying there baffled and troubled.

She returned with drinking water after dusk was fully down, her eyes swollen, her face flushed. He drank, pushed the dipper away, and said, "Missus Bartlett . . ."

"Close your eyes and go to sleep," she said in a dull tone, and left him again.

He watched opaque stars gradually brighten to the luminosity of diamond chips and heard coyotes somewhere behind him up the north hillside far beyond the woodshed. He saw the candles bring faint brightness inside the house, and he listened to the horses as they grazed in closer, perhaps inspired to do this by the passing pack of foraging coyotes.

He slept, awakened, and slept again, repeating this process until the cold arrived, which meant the night was far advanced. Then he slipped off into a deep slumber from which he did not awaken until a sliver of sunlight touched the top of the north hillside and made a silent explosion of brilliant light which flooded the meadow in less than a second.

His hip itched. He knew better than to move an arm to scratch and tried to ignore the itching by rolling his eyes to take in the familiar area of the broad, shallow valley.

He could move his head without causing the pain to flare up. Encouraged by that he moved his hand, then his arm, and finally wiggled his toes. That caused pain so he did not do it again, but it was very encouraging that he could at least move his arms. Still, he had no illusions about that; moving them was one thing, using them would be another. He did not put this theory to the test.

There was gray smoke rising from the stovepipe, which meant Elizabeth Bartlett was stirring. Walt was hungry, ravenously so in fact, which he thought was probably a good sign. He could touch his face; it was covered with two days' beard stubble. Until he made this discovery his appearance had not mattered. It still did not matter very much but he was conscious of it. His razor was down at the rooming house in Peralta.

That thought was followed by another one. He had left town day before yesterday. By now at least some of the people in Peralta would be wondering.

He yawned, turned to gaze in the direction of the willow-spring, and continued to look up there until he heard sounds from within the log house. Then he swung his attention to the rear door, but it did not open.

Some glistening big blue-tailed flies landed on the ground where his blood had soaked in and caked. He flicked his hand and they fled.

The sun climbed, cleared the eastern topout, and Elizabeth came out of the house with food and a bottle of water. She kept her eyes on the ground all the way to his pallet, leaned to put the dish and bottle beside him, and straightened up, still without looking at him, and returned to the house. She had not made a sound. He watched her disappear beyond the door, which was ajar, and frowned with bafflement.

CHAPTER 6

A Shock for Cutler

THE morning was well along and she still had not appeared as she had the previous morning to examine his wound and its bandaging. He had shade, he was progressing, his horse was completely content, and the itching had increased in his hip area so eventually he gingerly reached down there to scratch, and while the reaching brought no pain, the moment he touched the itching place there was pain.

He withdrew the hand and raised his eyes in the direction of the cabin and detected movement over along the south hillock, forgot completely about the itching, and narrowed his eyes in concentration.

It was a solitary rider, which was about all Cutler could make out because of sun-glare and distance. It could be someone from town looking for him, it could be . . . He raised his voice. "Missus Bartlett!"

She appeared in the doorway half in overhang shadow. He pointed. "Horseman coming."

That caused her to turn, gathering the shreds of her strength as she stepped beyond the house with a hand raised to shade her eyes. Then she began to walk very fast in the direction of the rider. Before she reached him she was running and had tears flowing down both cheeks. All Walt Cutler could see was her back and the way the mounted man hauled back to an abrupt stop at sight of her.

They spoke. Several times the mounted man glanced toward the house as they conversed, then he urged his horse ahead with Elizabeth hastening to keep abreast.

Finally Constable Cutler recognized the rider. His name was

Ned Eaton, they had met upon several occasions when Dr. Eaton had been summoned north to Peralta for illnesses and injuries. He was a short, stocky man with dark curly hair and a perpetually flattened set of lips. He could have been forty or fifty, or possibly even close to sixty—he had one of those smooth, lineless faces that appeared to defy the aging process.

As he was climbing down off one of Kelly O'Bryon's livery horses and saw the texas and the lumpy shape beneath it, his expression hardened into a look of grim resolve, which was characteristic of the man, but before he could approach Walt Cutler strong fingers gripped his arm, propelling him toward the house.

To Walt it seemed Dr. Eaton was in there for at least two hours before he walked out no longer wearing his coat, mopped sweat off his red face with a huge blue handkerchief, and stood in bright sunshine breathing deeply for a while before turning back in the direction of the open door without glancing in the constable's direction. The impression Walt got was of a man who had just escaped from something he was very grateful to be clear of.

Walt said, "Doctor."

The stocky man turned, then walked in the direction of the texas, and knelt looking into the shade with widening dark eyes. "Constable," he exclaimed in a voice made loud by astonishment. "The lady said a man . . . Constable, folks are wondering what happened to you down in Peralta." Without awaiting an explanation and acting as though he would not be very attentive if one were offered, Dr. Eaton lifted the blankets, considered the bandage, pursed his lips in a soundless whistle, and eased the blankets away as he leaned closer.

He removed the bandaging and made little humming sounds to himself as he examined and probed the wounds. Then he arose and without a word went back to the house for his little black bag.

When he returned he had a basin of water with him and a piece of homemade lye soap. He was kneeling as he said, "I will most likely hurt you, Constable—but you shouldn't even be alive so be thankful you can feel pain. That is a bullet wound. In here and—ah—out there . . . I told you this would hurt. I can dose you with laudanum and if I do you'll be like a dead weight. I will need your cooperation in moving so we won't use laudanum until this is over. All right?"

Clearly Dr. Eaton did not expect an answer and would not have heeded one if it had been given. He was an alert, confident individual and because his dedication required him to do everything possible for his patients regardless of pain, he had Walt Cutler gritting his teeth as he scissored away bits of torn flesh before moving on to disinfect both bullet holes before closing them as best he could. He dared not use gut stitches, even though the swelling was diminishing, so he used tape and, while applying it, warned the lawman of dire consequences if he moved around causing the closures to tear loose.

As he was re-dressing the holes he relaxed slightly, looked Cutler in the eye, and said, "Who shot you?"

Walt's gaze drifted to the cabin while he organized an answer, and Dr. Eaton, a very observant man, shook his head. "Not him, Constable." At Walt's look of doubt the medical man picked up a soggy cloth to cleanse his hands with as he said, "That man is dying of lung fever. I doubt if he's been able to walk without help for three or four months. He certainly has not been strong enough to hold a rifle, let alone shoulder and aim one, for a long time."

Walt stared.

Dr. Eaton finished cleaning his hands and sat back meeting Cutler's stare. In a lower tone he said, "I've seen it several dozen times. If Mr. Bartlett lasts another week it will be a miracle. Except for a powerful constitution he would not have lasted this long. He's been out of his head off and on for weeks, unable to stand or even to sit up for more than a few minues at a time . . . What makes you think he shot you?"

Walt's gaze drifted back to the house and he did not answer. Eventually he asked a question of his own. "Do they feel cold, Doctor?"

"All the time in the last stages. Cold and thirsty. As fast as they take water in they sweat it out. Constable, it's not a sight you'd want to see." Eaton also gazed in the direction of the house. "He's lucky. Very lucky. He don't know it now but he must have known it once. His wife is a remarkable woman. She's probably put in a year of agony and hard work not one woman out of a thousand could even imagine. Very lucky man, Constable . . . Well, you can't stay out here under this old piece of canvas, can you?"

Walt turned his head slowly. "I'm fine. Weak as hell, but until you arrived I didn't hurt unless I moved."

"You lost a lot of blood, Constable. In your condition it wouldn't take more than one good soaking in the rain to bring on pneumonia and you'd be too puny to fight it off." Dr. Eaton studied the lawman's face for a moment then said, "What were you doing out here anyway," and before Walt could have answered he also said, "Maybe whoever shot you thought you were Mr. Bartlett; that happens now and then, doesn't it? Settlers, I mean, getting shot for taking up open range."

Eaton grunted up to his feet and turned to study his surroundings. He had seen this kind of poverty many times. "Why do they do it?" he said aloud, but to himself, then became practical again. "You shouldn't be in that house. I'll tell folks in town where you are and they can come out with a rig that has good springs under it and haul you back to town where you can hire some woman to look after you . . . Do you want some laudanum now?"

Walt shook his head; the doctor was beginning to annoy him. It was the older man's impersonal attitude. He wanted to tell Eaton he should have been a preacher. Instead he said, "How long before I can stand up?"

Eaton's expression turned dour. "If I had a penny for every time I've been asked that I'd be a rich man . . . At the very least, two months, Constable." He pursed his lips. "I know your kind; as soon as my back is turned you'll do something foolish. I can't be driving up here every week or so. But I can warn you that if you get an infection or if you overdo it in your weakened condition, you could very well die. They can look after you down in—"

"No," Walt said shortly. "I don't need a wagon ride to Peralta. I'll be all right where I am."

Dr. Eaton's cheeks puffed out and reddened. "Constable, that woman's got to bury her man in a week or so, meanwhile she doesn't need another invalid to sweat over—not in her condition. She's worn out. It wouldn't surprise me one bit if she came down sick. She is ready to drop in her tracks. You're going to be a burden to everyone for a long time—don't add to her pain and weariness . . . Constable, you hear me?"

Cutler was like stone for a long time before nodding his head. "Yeah," he said flatly. "Send the wagon for me . . . Doctor?"

"Yes."

"A week?"

Dr. Eaton thought a moment before saying, "At the most a week. Maybe tonight or tomorrow. Once they no longer eat . . . He doesn't weigh seventy-five pounds, Constable, and I'd guess his healthy weight to be about two hundred pounds. They go fast once they get down this far."

"When you get back to Peralta look up Fred Tower. He owns the harness works and tannery. Tell him to bring O'Bryon the liveryman with him in the wagon. Tell him to bring digging tools. Remember the names, Tower and O'Bryon. And don't tell anyone else. Tell Tower and O'Bryon not to tell anyone else." After speaking Walt looked steadily at the medical practitioner. "Plenty of straw in the wagon-bed—and some whiskey."

Dr. Eaton's gaze was sardonic. "Tower, O'Bryon, digging tools, straw, and whiskey. Sure you haven't forgot anything?"

Walt's mouth flattened, his eyes hardened. Eaton knew the signs and picked up his black bag and walked over to the house.

A light breeze brisked up from the north, which was welcome. Out where the horses were idly standing switching their tails at flies, one animal flung up its head and stared intently northeastward, moving its head slowly as whatever it had caught sight of moved southward along the wind-scourged ridge.

Walt glanced out there, saw the horse, and followed out its line of vision until he also saw movement up the slope slightly northward of the willow-spring and farther back.

It was a rider. He could feel hair rising along the back of his neck. The distance was too great but he was sure the horseman was looking down from his higher place toward the log house in its sunbright clearing.

Where several second-growth pines were flourishing amid a clump of rotting large pine stumps, the horseman halted, still facing southward but sitting crooked in the saddle as he studied the cabin and its surrounding area. He no doubt saw three horses where there were only supposed to be two, and he probably saw Dr. Eaton's livery animal dozing in shade on the north side of the house. Whether he could make sense out of the piece of old canvas stretched above something lumpy on the ground at that distance was doubtful, but he should have had no trouble picking up indications that the house was not abandoned, that, in fact it seemed to have more people down there around it than it had had before.

He kneed the horse, emerged from the little trees, and turned off northward out of sight down the far side of the hill.

Walt was still looking up there when Dr. Eaton emerged from the house shrugging into his black coat. He was chewing an unlighted cigar. He eyed Cutler for a moment, then walked over to him. "I told her they'd be coming to take you off her hands. That's all I told her . . . Constable, when it's all over it might be a good idea if someone could talk her into leaving this place. Maybe moving into Peralta or going back wherever she came from . . . I suspect the trains going back east must carry almost as many of these people as they bring out here. Remember what I told you; be very careful. Don't push yourself. It will help if you'll eat lots of rare beef and raw eggs . . ."

Walt said, "There are three cartwheels in my pants pocket,

Doctor," and Eaton removed his soggy cigar, regarded its unlighted end, plugged it back between his teeth, and said, "Send it to me, Constable." Then he walked around into the shade where his horse was standing, scrambled into the saddle, reined around to the front of the house, and picked up the ruts which he would follow all the way back to Peralta.

The only sounds for a while were made by the doctor's horse and they did not last long. After they died out there was no sound at all.

Walt reached down to touch his bandage. There was no pain so he pressed a little harder. This time he got a painful response but it was not as bad a pain as before. He considered easing up onto one elbow simply to test his strength. Elizabeth appeared in the shaded doorway facing in his direction. He wanted to say something, could not think of anything that might be appropriate—maybe because there wasn't anything appropriate to the moment—and wisely said nothing.

She brought him a fresh water bottle. When she leaned to place it beside the pallet and pick up the bottle he had emptied earlier, she said, "I didn't mean to neglect you."

"You didn't. I was fine. They'll be after me in the morning with a wagon."

She nodded her head, straightening up without looking at his face. "Yes. I'm sorry I couldn't do better."

"You did more than Dr. Eaton did—and didn't hurt half as much." He took down a big breath. "I didn't know your husband was sick."

"I know you didn't or you wouldn't have accused him of shooting you . . . We're a long way out, Constable. We never went down to Peralta unless we absolutely had to. No one could have told you except maybe the Mortons. They took up land about twelve miles from here across the White family's range. They drove over to visit for a few days last autumn. They knew."

He wanted her to look him in the eye but she remained standing with her gaze fixed upon the ground across the pallet westward. She turned finally and walked heavily back to the house, the little welcome breeze blowing lightly against her skirt and head. It made her very dark red-copper hair twist in coils to capture and hold the sunlight.

CHAPTER 7

"Right Where You Are!"

THE following morning the sun was still climbing when Walt heard a wagon approaching from around in front of the house, probably following the ruts. He knew who it would be and for an additional few moments lay totally relaxed studying that easterly hilltop where the rider had been. There was nothing up there nor had he expected there to be.

Elizabeth came outside when the rig moved down the south side of the house, then turned into the rear yard and halted. It was a fairly new light spring wagon. The green paint was just beginning to show wear. The team were large, sleek sorrels, a matched pair. Walt knew them and the wagon. The sorrels were Kelly O'Bryon's particular pride and joy. He did not hire them out; they were kept for his private use and for pulling his black hearse with the glass windows on both sides.

Kelly was driving; when he climbed down he did so on the near side. Lanky Fred Tower came down on the off side still wearing a coat. They both stared over where Walt Cutler was gazing back at them. Elizabeth raised a chapped hand to brush back a coil of red-copper hair when she asked if they would care for hot coffee. Both men gazed at her as though she had been invisible before, then Fred wagged his head. "No thanks, ma'am. We ate couple of hours back in town . . . We came for Mr. Cutler. We got blankets and straw in the wagon and—"

She nodded, turning slowly. Walt introduced them, then Fred and Kelly walked up and looked down. "You look like somethin' a dog would drag in," O'Bryon stated soberly. "What happened, Walt?"

Cutler looked from the woman to the house, then back toward

his friends. "Got shot," he said tersely. "We can talk on the drive back . . . Missus Bartlett, I owe you more than I can repay."

She said nothing, merely showed the faintest of smiles. Then she addressed Tower and O'Bryon. "You must be very careful. He lost a lot of blood . . . Maybe I could help."

The tanner smiled indulgently. "Right nice of you to offer, lady, but we can manage."

She stood a moment longer, then went over to the house without another word and Fred Tower leaned down to say, quietly, "Dr. Eaton said her husband's dying, can't last more'n another day or so. We know about Sexton, that rangeman who got killed out here. Everybody in town knows. Is that why you come out here—to haul her husband to the jailhouse?"

Walt pondered his reply before offering it. "Well, at first that was my reason, yes, but Eaton says her husband's too weak with the lung fever to even walk—has been that way for weeks."

Lanky Fred Tower bobbed his head. "Then he didn't kill Mack Kelso's rider, did he?"

Walt looked a long time at the tanner, long enough for Fred to redden slightly and straighten up as he briskly said, "Kelly, if you'd drive the wagon a little closer . . ."

Kelly did not drive it, he led the horses up beside the texas and they brought the wagon with them. Without a word he freed the chain and lowered the tailgate. He stood speculatively eyeing Cutler and his bedding. "Where was you hit?" he asked, and, when Walt told him, O'Bryon said, "I thought it'd be something like that. Fred, we can't just take him by the ankles and shoulders, he's got to be kept straight."

Fred required time to consider the situation so he delved for his plug of cured molasses and gnawed off a corner of it while gazing around the yard. He laconically reported that there was no wooden plank they could insert beneath the constable. The nearest thing to it would be a piece of the rough siding off the woodshed.

Kelly smiled. "I got something."

Fred looked skeptical. "What?"

"I brought along a heavy plank. It's under the hay in the wagon. The sawbones give me the idea. Lend a hand with it, Fred."

Before moving away Fred Tower threw Constable Cutler an exasperated look and rolled his eyes. For the first time in several days Walt wanted to laugh.

With the best of intentions they got the wide, thick plank under Cutler by grunting a lot and concentrating on what they were doing—like Dr. Eaton, without much concern for the man gritting his teeth as they pushed him atop the plank. Although Walt was a large, heavy man they had no difficulty lifting him, carrying him to the wagon-bed, and with as much gentleness as a tanner of hides and a liveryman would ever possess, pushed, shoved, and heaved until they had Walt on his plank into the wagon.

His upper lip and forehead were beaded with sweat by the time they climbed up to make a cushion for him of the loose straw and draped two blankets over him. Then they smiled at one another for having handled things so well before climbing back to the ground where Kelly chained up the tailgate.

Fred Tower remembered something. He went up to the front of the wagon and dug among the old sacks beneath the seat, found the bottle, and brought it back to Walt. It was the first whiskey Cutler had tasted in days. He swallowed twice, let them take back the bottle, and watched as they both also had a couple of swallows.

The liquor had an almost instantaneous effect on Walt. His eyes brightened, his tense body loosened, and the sun became much brighter. He let go with a rattling loud sigh, turned his head slightly toward the log house, and did not hear O'Bryon when he offered reassurance that he would avoid potholes and ruts wherever he could, but it was a long drive back to town over uneven ground so maybe Walt had ought to keep the whiskey bottle.

O'Bryon placed it in the straw beside Cutler's blankets and

walked resolutely forward to climb to the wagon-seat and pick up the lines.

Walt watched the cabin as the wagon began to move but Elizabeth did not appear. He heard Kelly and Fred talking as the wagon made a circle and headed out of the neck beside the ruts.

Kelly was a good teamster, but as he had warned, there would be bad places. Walt's pain came sharply each time they encountered a bump or went down a swale and jarred up its far side. The hitch had twice as much power as this kind of a light rig required, which meant they moved without straining in their collars, covering ground at a strong pace.

Fred leaned down once to see how the constable was managing, and when their eyes met, Fred grinned. "Folks in town ain't talkin' about much else except you goin' somewhere after a killer. There's been some worryin' and a lot of speculating. Last night at the Horseshoe, Gus Heinz was growling about the Whites; said he wouldn't put it past 'em to waylay you if you was bringin' in that settler who killed their rider with a rock."

Walt said nothing. People always talked; most of them had tongues that hinged in the middle and wagged at both ends. They jarred over a half-hidden rock and Walt fisted both hands against the pain. Kelly twisted to look apologetic but said nothing because there was nothing to say; he was doing the best he could.

Heat was coming by the time they were rounding the low hillock south of the neck, with open country dead ahead all the way to town. Walt saw the shadowy place where he had watched Elizabeth Bartlett heading for Peralta on that big pudding-footed horse. It meant that they were well on their way, but Walt did not see it as a landmark, he thought of the handsome woman with red-copper hair and great dark rings beneath her eyes.

When they were passing over relatively level grassland Walt said, "How the heck is she going to bury him—alone by herself out there?"

Fred twisted again to look downwards into the bed of the

wagon. "Well, we brought digging tools. Maybe we should have left them."

That statement exasperated Cutler. "Tools don't dig graves, Fred, people do. Men, not worn-out heartsick widow-women."

Tower shifted his cud, continued to regard the invalid, and finally made a suggestion. "All right; after we get you settled and all, we can come back out here and dig the hole. Walt, if he don't die for days we can't just set out there like buzzards on a fence waitin' for an old cow to die."

Walt was already thinking along a different line. "When we reach town I'd take it kindly if you fellers would find Missus Sargent the midwife and tell her I'd like to see her at my place at the rooming house."

Fred nodded slowly, chewed, expectorated aside, then said, "What for?" They had been talking about digging a grave and Walt had said women didn't do things like that.

"I'll hire her to go out and be with Missus Bartlett. She could ride back with you fellers when you go to dig the grave."

Fred masticated a moment in silence, then squared around on the seat. He and Kelly O'Bryon exchanged a long, blank look.

The south hillock which hid Bartlett's meadow from view was dropping back. To the west where there were a number of those low, thick lifts and rises, but with trees growing on their slopes as opposed to the old stumps on the Bartletts' low hill. Fred was dozing, Kelly was driving with slack lines watching several pronghorns which had either heard the wagon or had seen it and were now running toward the timbered westerly slope faster than the finest racehorse could run, tails up, white rumps showing.

Walt was sweating, more now from the heat than from pain. He would have liked a drink of cold water but said nothing and watched a pair of red-tailed hawks making mock sweeps at one another high overhead.

Ahead and to the left where a spit of pines came down off the diminishing end of the same hill which protected the east end of the Bartlett place—the same hill where the willow-spring was, where the White outfit's rider had been killed—slight movement appeared among tree shadows. The sun barely penetrated to the round over there and in the places where it did penetrate there was a mottled spread of diffused light, like camouflage.

The wagon was about a mile away but traveling toward the lower end of the spit where it came down to a *V*. It would pass within a hundred or so yards of the tip of the *V*.

Kelly's antelope disappeared in a flash of white rumps where they reached timber, and Fred snored, so Kelly dug him in the ribs with an elbow. The red-tailed hawks, like all their kind, widened their circling sweeps even while playing, until they were soaring above the ridge of that same timber hill where the antelope had gone.

A rear wheel dropped unexpectedly through the roof of a prairie dog's hole and jarred up out of it bringing an un-uttered curse to Walt's lips. He tensed until the pain passed, then raised up slightly to make an unkind remark and saw quick, murky movement off the left and on ahead where that tapering spit of pine trees was. He forgot about the jostling and squinted hard in an effort to make out shapes. When he eventually spoke he said, "Kelly, watch over yonder among those pine trees. There's something big in there. Just keep watching; it's not moving now but it *was* moving."

Both men on the seat sat a little straighter as they studied the trees. Fred said it was probably an old sow bear rooting among stumps for grubs. Kelly said nothing but he changed course a little, angling more southward because, if that was a bear and his horses picked up the scent, he was going to have to use all the tricks in his bag of them to avoid a runaway.

In aggravation he said, "You'd think with all the blowhards around town who're forever tellin' what mighty hunters they are, they'd be able to keep bears from gettin' this close to town."

"Hey," Fred exclaimed suddenly, drawing up straighter on the seat. "That's riders . . . Two that I can see . . . Now I can't see 'em. They . . ." The tanner's voice had an edge of apprehension to it. "Kelly . . . turn off, turn plumb away. I don't like this. They've seen us sure enough. They know we're out here so why don't they just ride out like anyone else would do?"

Walt and O'Bryon both had something to divide their attention. Walt had his pain and O'Bryon had his team, but there was no way to avoid sensing Fred Tower's sudden concern, and they had known Tower for years, he was not someone who spooked easily. Walt raised a hand to the low sideboard in order to steady himself. He had no idea who that would be over in the pine-shadows but he did know that at least one man had been watching the Bartlett place because he had seen him doing it miles northward along that same hill.

Kelly snugged back one line to make the big horses begin a wide turn southward, which would be directly away from the trees, but the wagon was still quite close. Much closer than it had been when Fred had first raised the alarm.

A single horseman emerged from the trees at a walk. He faced the wagon, did not raise a casual arm in the customary range salute, and had his course set to intercept the wagon at a point some fifty or so yards ahead.

All three watchers tried to identify the man, but aside from a hat brim-shaded face he was not close enough. They knew he was a rangeman from general appearance, but that was all they knew.

A second horseman walked his animal out of the spit of pines, but this man did not go completely beyond the tree-shade before reining to a dead stop facing the wagon.

Fred said, "Damn!"

The farthest horseman had stopped up ahead at the point where he would have intercepted the wagon and raised a gloved hand as he called out.

"Hold it. Stop right where you are. Keep your hands in sight."

The rider dropped his arm, slid a Winchester from its saddleboot, and with almost casual behavior, dismounted and sank to one knee with the Winchester in both hands.

Kelly raised his foot to set the binders but made no attempt to loop the lines around the brake handle, which he normally would have done. He wanted his hands high enough to be in plain sight. From the side of his mouth he said, "Walt, you got a gun?"

Cutler did not even know what had become of his weapons. "No, and if either one of you do have, for Chrissake don't reach for them. There's another one back in the trees, that makes three of them. Don't do a thing but what they tell you."

CHAPTER 8

The Face of Death

THE distant men did not leave Walt and his friends in doubt for long. The kneeling man facing them in the shadow of his saddlehorse with the Winchester loosely aimed scarcely had to raise his voice to be heard across the intervening distance.

"You boys on the seat—throw down your guns."

Fred sounded more bitter than indignant when he called back. "We aren't armed. We just came out here to—"

"Shut your mouth!"

Fred obeyed, his dark eyes smoldering.

"Now then," stated the kneeling man. "You two climb down . . . Be careful . . . climb down, go around in back, let down the tailgate, and yank that son of a gun out of there. You hear me? Yank him out, dump him on the ground, then you two get back up and drive away. You understand me? Keep right on driving. Don't even look back . . . Now get down!"

For five seconds none of the men with the wagon moved. The order had astonished them, but when the surprise passed indignation took over and Kelly O'Bryon bitterly protested. "We got a hurt man in the wagon bed, he's been shot and—"

Walt whispered quickly as that kneeling man's saddlegun began to rise. "Kelly! Do what he said! Those bastards are going to kill somebody."

Fred snarled softly from the side of his mouth. "Yeah. You, Walt . . . I wish I had my carbine."

The rider, who had been looking on from pine-shade, spoke next. "You're goin' to do it," he called, "or we're goin' to leave all three of you out here. *Drag him out of that wagon!*"

Walt whispered again, more insistently this time. "Do it; do what they say."

Kelly's face was red as he leaned to loop the lines then start down. Fred Tower's jaw was clamped in an ugly expression as he too stepped from the wheel-hub to the ground, paused to gaze at the man with the carbine, then turned his back to help with the tailgate. Kelly was sweating. "Who are they?" he asked Walt. "What the heck . . ." He let the chain trickle slowly through his fingers.

Fred spared a moment to lean and look ahead. A third horseman was emerging from the spit of timber. He had a carbine across his lap, and with Fred watching he up-ended it, sank the weapon into its boot, then raised both hands to tie a dark cloth over his face. Fred squinted. "Highwaymen? Walt, this don't make one lick of sense, we're not haulin' gold."

O'Bryon, who had been thinking hard, said, "They know that. They want Walt. Fred, we can't leave him here."

The kneeling man arose and with his reins hanging from one set of gloved fingers walked forward very slowly, leading the horse as he settled the Winchester in the curve of his shoulder. They heard him cock it.

Walt said, "Lift me down, Fred! Pick up the plank!"

Kelly and Fred climbed up, eased Walt over the tailgate, then climbed down to lift him out. The man with the cocked gun said, "Get him out. Drop it. Hurry up with it!"

They did not hurry; they bent down and very gently placed Walt on his plank upon the ground. As they straightened up facing the horsemen with clenched fists and squared shoulders Walt said, "Get back up there and drive away. Do what I say. What's the sense of tryin' to buck three armed men when you don't even have a stick? Kelly! Get up there!"

They looked down at the sweaty, whiskery, drawn face of Constable Cutler. They were not going to do it. Come hell or high water they were not going to abandon Cutler. They would not have done it even if he'd been able to stand on his own two feet.

Both the horsemen from the trees were now masked. They walked their horses toward the rear of the wagon taking down coiled lass ropes as they approached. It required no great knowledge of range ways to see that these were experienced ropers. Nor was their purpose in shaking out little loops incomprehensible to the pair of men standing above their friend at the tailgate.

That third man remained about seventy-five feet from the team horses slightly to their right, cocked carbine aimed in the direction of O'Bryon and Tower.

Walt, who heard walking horses, tried to look backwards through the wheel-spokes. He knew those two from the trees were coming but was unable to see anything until they were alongside the rig, then all he saw was shod hooves and horse legs.

He knew what was happening when the first noose snaked ahead with hissing speed. He saw Kelly lurch to duck his head, and heard one of the horsemen grunt as he took dallics and whirled away. Kelly was jerked violently against the wagon, bounced off, and while trying to run with the rope, lost his balance and was dragged.

Fred Tower stood like a stone statue facing the other roper as he said, "If I ever get my hands on you I'll break every bone in your body." He would not give the roper the satisfaction of seeing him cringe to try to duck clear. The noose settled almost gently. Walt saw the slack taken up, but this time the horseman did not whirl away in a stiff trot; he turned slowly, holding his dallies and riding at a walk, forcing Fred Tower's stiff legs to bend as he was led away.

There was no talking. In fact after his friends had been taken away Walt could hear nothing for a long time, not until someone wearing spurs came slowly down the off side of the wagon. He turned to watch, saw the boots, the spurs, the horse being led along, and knew which one this was: the man with the carbine, the rangerider who was going to kill him.

He was in physical pain, his mouth and throat were dry, the whiskey had long since ceased to have any strengthening effect.

In fact he now felt more bone-tired than before he'd drunk the stuff.

The horseman came around the wagon and looked down. His face was covered from the bridge of the nose to below the chin with a faded bandana handkerchief. He was holding the cocked Winchester tilted downward with one gloved finger curled inside the trigger guard.

Walt looked upwards. The man's tawny brown eyes were very slowly widening. He stared at Walt for a long time without moving. From what seemed like a great distance but which was only a short reach from the front of the wagon someone called impatiently.

"Get it over with! Hurry up, get it over with!"

The rangeman seemed too preoccupied to have heard. He stared steadily at Cutler for what seemed an eternity, then looked inside the wagon, even used the carbine barrel to poke in the straw with. He straightened back and stared downward again and when Walt thought he was going to speak, the rider turned suddenly, dropped the carbine into its boot, and swung into the saddle reining toward the front of the wagon where his companions were glaring from angry faces.

He jerked his head. "Take off the ropes. Let 'em go."

The man who had Fred Tower in his noose wrinkled his face until his eyes were nearly hidden. "What is wrong with you? Why didn't you . . . Here, hold this rope an' I'll finish the bastard."

"No! You two listen to me! It's not him. Now let them bastards go and let's get the heck out of here."

One of the ropers leaned on his saddlehorn, staring. "Not him? What are you—"

"Gawddammit," roared the man who had held the Winchester. "Let 'em go! Now! *We're settin' out here in plain sight.* Take off them ropes and hurry up at it!"

The pair of ropers eased up, giving slack enough for Fred and Kelly to free themselves. After flinging the ropes down to be coiled by the riders, they both stood there watching the horsemen make a run for it back in the direction of that spit of timber.

Kelly massaged his shoulders with a sore arm encased in a torn sleeve where he had been dragged behind a trotting horse. Fred let go a ragged breath, turned, and without a word went back behind the wagon.

Walt looked up at him.

Fred simply sat down in the grass with meager shade from the wagon partially covering him, and fished for his plug of chewing tobacco.

Kelly arrived and also sat down while regarding Walt Cutler and at the same time rubbing his sore shoulder. He spoke first. "That feller who came back here to shoot you rode up where we was and told the other two you weren't the one—whatever that meant—but thank gawd you wasn't."

Fred chewed, nursed his bleak, cold fury, and had nothing to say for a while. He was slow to anger and just as slow recovering from anger. Right now he was recovering.

Walt needed a drink. They all did, so Kelly fished in the straw until he had the bottle and came back to sit behind the wagon in skimpy shade, out in the middle of nowhere, as the bottle was passed around.

Perhaps the whiskey, perhaps the passage of time and the diminishing shock and surprise, or perhaps just that his anger was down to coals made Fred Tower expectorate out into the sunlight before he said, "Did you fellers recognize any of those men?"

Kelly, who did very little business with stockmen and only knew a few by sight from seeing them around town, shook his head.

Walt said nothing, his face was shaded by the wagon, and as his friends waited for a response he eyed Fred Tower. "How about you?"

Tower squinted against distant sunsmash while answering in his deliberate way. "Lots of rangemen come into the harness shop. Some to have saddles or bridles patched up, some to have new spur leathers made, things like that." He shortened his view to Walt and Kelly. "The one that had me at the end of his rope was wearing hand-carved spur leathers from my place. A Mexican makes them for me. He does real fine work."

Kelly was impatient. "Never mind all that. What's the name of that rider; does he work for the Whites? That's the nearest big outfit."

Fred looked uncomfortable. "I don't know who bought them. I just recognized them is all. When we get back to town I'll see what I can dig up, but the trouble is if someone pays cash I hand over the leathers, take his money, and that's that."

After a long moment of quiet Cutler pushed up into a half leaning position looking intently at Tower and O'Bryon. "Something that's stuck in my craw since I got shot was—why me? I can tell you for a fact he was a long ways off when I walked around the back of the Bartlett house." Walt paused. The idea that had come to him needed careful articulation and, because he was not sure how he had arrived at it, he had to proceed slowly.

"He was up near where Sexton was killed. White range is on the other side of that hill. He saw me and took his time before shooting. He saw me go down for sure and he saw the doctor come in yesterday morning and saw you fellers drive in today with the wagon and load me into it and start for town."

Kelly rolled his eyes. "Will you just spit it out, Walt?"

Cutler looked directly at O'Bryon when he resumed speaking. "Did you know that settler out there was dying?"

Kelly shook his head. "How would I have known? They never came to town that I know of."

Walt nodded. "I didn't know it either. I guess no one else knew it hereabouts except some other settlers and they live over beyond White's range. One of you asked me if I went out there day before yesterday to arrest Bartlett for suspicion of having killed Sexton. That's exactly why I went out there and until Dr. Eaton showed up yesterday I still didn't know Bartlett was on the edge of dying. He couldn't have killed Sexton."

Tower and O'Bryon were gazing blankly at Walt. He pointed with one hand in the direction those rangemen had taken. "They didn't know it either—but someone thought he hadn't killed me when he tried his bushwack, and waited until this morning to make sure I got killed—only he thought the man you were taking to town was Bartlett. He thought he'd shot Bartlett. He was too far off to know the difference . . . Just now, when that feller with the Winchester looked at me he looked like he couldn't believe his eyes. He didn't expect to see me, he expected to see the settler, and I think if it had been Bartlett he'd have killed him on the spot. When he saw it wasn't Bartlett he didn't know what to do. He just stood there until someone yelled, then he mounted up and rode away."

Fred Tower needed a fresh chew in order to sort all this out in his mind and Kelly O'Bryon stood up and looked up ahead at his peacefully dozing big horses, then hunkered down and reached for the whiskey bottle. When finished with it he planted it firmly on the ground in front of Walt and blew out a fiery breath.

"Damn," he said in a long sigh of sound. "Walt, it *had* to be riders from the White place. It had to be men who knew Sexton, who maybe have been riding with him this season and liked him . . . Maybe Mack Kelso, even . . ."

Fred suddenly sat bolt upright, his jaws motionless around the cud of molasses-cured Kentucky twist. "Jesus!" he exclaimed, his normally squinted dark eyes popping wide open. "They'll go back. They'll head for the cabin. If you wasn't Bartlett then they know he's got to be at the log house!"

Fred was on his feet before either of his companions moved. He barked at O'Bryon. "Get hold of the other end of this damned plank. Move, Kelly, move!"

Kelly sprang for the other end of the plank with Walt Cutler clinging to both sides of it and, as they lifted him over the tailgate and heaved, he let out a groan. Kelly stopped pushing and faced Fred. "We can't take him along. Pull him back out. The ride will likely bust him open. Pull him out, Fred."

Walt raised his voice to them through the pain. "Leave me here. Get up there and turn those horses around, Kelly."

"Walt, it'll kill you!"

Cutler swore fiercely. "You idiot, they'll kill her and her

husband. Latch the tailgate, and turn this wagon around."
Fred and O'Bryon stared at Walt, then at each other, and Fred
finally reached for the tailgate chain.

It did not occur to any of them that going back to the neck
was very probably going to result in more than just the settlers
getting shot to death—because none of them had weapons.

CHAPTER 9

A Drive to Remember

THE actual distance back to the neck was not very great. O'Bryon's concentration on picking the least jarring way toward Peralta had used up a good part of the morning and it had not really advanced their progress greatly, so the return trip did not involve a great distance.

Also, a unique fact about spring-wagons was that they rode rougher at a dead walk than they did at high speed. Kelly's big powerful harness horses had been feeling up to snuff all morning, had fretted at being compelled to poke along, so when he made a big turn and got them lined out back over their own tracks, and slackened the lines as he whistled them up, both animals went up into their collar-pads, actually lifting the light wagon off the ground for an inch or two before it came down with the wheels spinning. That initial jar was hard but none of the passengers had time to gasp because the big animals had the wagon tongue straight between them. Either one of them could have pulled the light rig by himself; both of them pulling together had the wagon skimming over curing tall grass as though it were weightless.

Fred almost swallowed his cud. He was clinging to the seat with both big hands. Kelly was sitting back, boots braced against the low dashboard, grinning like an idiot. For O'Bryon, the lifelong horseman, life did not get any better for a man if he could sit behind handsome, big, sound, young horses and feel the power of their muscles working at high speed.

Walt ground his teeth at the first jarring lunge of the wagon, but afterwards did not think of pain as he watched the land whip away behind the tailgate. Like Fred Tower, he reached for something to cling to although there really was no need; he had green sideboards on both sides, the tailgate beyond his feet, and the headboard and seat in the opposite direction. Nor was the ride as bad now as it had been going toward Peralta earlier, perhaps in part because he was not thinking of the pain. He was too worried about the rig flipping over, which would not happen in any case as long as Kelly held his horses in a direct line, and the wheels did not strike a large rock, of which there were none on the ride back toward the neck. It was all good, deep soil as Walt himself had observed at other, less trying, times.

Fred risked freeing one hand to yank down the front of his hat and to twist and look down into the wagon bed. Walt looked back. Neither one of them said a word.

Kelly had the tapering-down west end of the south hillock in sight as he began to take up the slack and begin a very wide curving turn. Under a less experienced teamster the wagon could have been turned over, but O'Bryon was one of the best drivers in the country. He crossed the ruts to let his animals go out almost a half mile in their very gradual turn.

Fred watched with his heart in his throat, and although Walt could feel the rig angling around, he could not raise up to look out; he too waited for the disaster which never arrived.

Kelly completed his big turn, aimed the horses directly up into the neck with the log house clearly visible in the distance, and he threw back his head and laughed. The danger of an accident was past. Fred glared at him and cried above the rush of wind and the noise of horses and harness. "You're crazy! Slow those horses down!"

Kelly's face was shiny and red as he shot Tower a gloating leer and began to ease back on the lines. The horses had had their miles-long run, had got the snuffiness out of their systems, and were perfectly willing to slacken off.

Fred turned again to look down at Constable Cutler. "You all right?" he exclaimed.

Walt looked up at the strained, leathery face. "No, I'm not all

right. Either one of those tapes came off or else I wet my pants
. . . Can you see the house?"

"Yeah. Don't see anyone up there though."

"Around in back," Walt said, reaching for a sideboard to
hoist himself up slightly.

Tower admonished him. "Lie back. You can't see from there
anyway." He faced forward on the seat, dark eyes in their
customary squint again as he leaned slightly as though this
would help him see better.

Fred had his sweating big horses down to an ungainly trot,
which annoyed Fred, who growled at him to drop down to a
walk because a trot would jar the guts out of Walt. Kelly obeyed
and they both concentrated on trying to find movement up
where the log house sat in its wide meadow. What they did not
notice, and probably wouldn't have thought anything about if
they had noticed it, was that there was no smoke rising from the
stovepipe.

As the team plodded along Kelly said, "Awful quiet up
there."

Walt pushed up into a leaning position ignoring the pain this
caused—and unmindful that in fact although there was pain it
was not as bad as it had been. "Angle," he said to O'Bryon.
"Angle off to the left, Kelly, so's we can see around back."

Fred was stuffing cured molasses into his face when he
scowled about this. "Those bastards got carbines. Stay as far to
the left as you can."

O'Bryon dutifully swung so wide over the meadow he
seemed to be aiming for the far sidehill of that low hillock over
there. They had completed about half the distance when the
unmistakable, flat sound of a gunshot carried clearly out to
them. All heads craned to the right looking for gunpowder
smoke. There should have been some but they did not see it.

But the gunshot verified what had galvanized Fred Tower in
the first place; those gunmen had indeed come back here in
their unrelenting hunt of the man they thought had killed their
friend.

Fred growled. "Sons of guns."

Kelly was more practical. "Where are they?"

The wagon had cleared the south side of the log house and was now in plain sight of anyone around in back. It was also a considerable distance away, perhaps not quite out of saddlegun range but certainly far enough from the buildings to make aiming at the two men on the seat difficult, and hitting them unlikely unless, as Walt said, one of those rangemen was the fellow who had shot him from an even greater distance.

Kelly stopped the rig, set the binders, looped his lines, and frowned. "I never been fond of guns but right this minute I'd trade a good horse for one."

Fred and Walt said nothing; they were trying intently to locate even just one of those rangemen. Another gunshot sounded; O'Bryon instinctively flinched although there was no sound to indicate the wagon had been the target.

Fred suddenly jabbed with an outstretched arm. "In the woodshed. See that smoke?"

Walt and Kelly peered in that direction and at the same time there was another gunshot, louder and deeper this time. It had not come from the shed; they watched the puff of dirty smoke blossom along the back of the log house. Fred was the first to speak after this. "If that settler's so sick . . . he's puttin' up a pretty good fight."

Walt answered shortly. "That's not him, that's her. Sure as I'm sitting here."

Fred looked back and downward, pushing sweat off his face with a sleeve as he dryly said, "Well, if it's the lady-settler, they're goin' to play hell smokin' her out—and we near killed ourselves getting back here."

Walt pointed toward the south wall of the house. "If we could get over yonder . . . They can't see around there. If we could get over there without them—"

"What are you talking about?" O'Bryon demanded. "They could see anyone running from here toward the house, and even if we got there—then what; throw rocks?"

The shooter inside the log house was using a rifle, not a carbine. The noise was much more menacing when the weapon was fired. Also, its range was much greater and its slug was larger. Shooting from the house no farther than the woodshed with that gun was like killing flies with a shotgun, and quite clearly the men hiding in the shed knew all of this because not only were they invisible inside the dark shed but each time they fired it seemed to be from a different position.

Walt took time off during a lull to peel back his blankets, raise his dirty, ragged shirt, and peek beneath Dr. Eaton's bandaging. He was certain he was bleeding.

He wasn't. The tapes were in place, there was no red stain anywhere except on the tapes. He wondered why he had thought he had felt wet blood and recovered himself without arriving at an answer.

There had been a long lull in the gun battle going back even before Walt had taken time out to examine himself, and now it continued.

He made a guess. "They can see us out here and they haven't been able to shoot themselves inside the house. From the way they acted back where they stopped us I'd guess they don't like having to wait."

Fred Tower dourly grunted, spat, reached to yank his hat still lower above his squinty eyes, and said nothing. Neither did Kelly O'Bryon whose shirtfront was beginning to show dark sweat stains.

Now it was possible for the three of them to think more calmly and speculatively. If the fight was to be resumed someone had to start it and no one was doing that. The rifle inside the house had fired last; it had seemed to fire only when one of the men with saddleguns fired first. That, Kelly said, satisfied him. It had to be the woman: "A man wouldn't have been content to sit in there and wait for someone to shoot at him first."

Fred turned a jaundiced look upon the man sharing the wagon-seat with him, spat, and turned away without uttering a word. Kelly's face reddened.

Walt had to brace against the sideboard. He had begun to grow weak from leaning without support for so long, but his mind was not tiring, just his body. How, he asked himself, were those gunmen going to bust out of the shed on their horses without getting shot at as they tried to race away? Perhaps, as O'Bryon had surmised, they would not be shot at.

He was right—and he was wrong. When the rangemen finally concluded what must have been a stiff argument, during which time they did not resume the fight, one of them suddenly appeared as a flash of movement. He sprang into the sunshine and whipped down the west side of the woodshed. He was visible for less than five seconds.

There was no shot from the house.

Fred spat without taking his eyes off the shed. "Now another'll try it," he guessed and was correct. The second man repeated the first one's dash. Fred sighed and eased back against the seat. "Had their horses tied out back—of course," he said sourly. "Most likely come up onto the house from the north, keepin' the shed between them and the house . . . I've known a lot of rangemen, gents, and can't say as I've ever known very many I thought was very smart, but those sons of guns did a pretty fair job of figuring things."

Kelly snorted. "They sure did; stopped us to kill a man who wasn't within five miles of us, then came back here to kill him, and didn't have the sense to just maybe ride up pretendin' to be friendly so's they could get inside the house."

Fred was unperturbed. He pointed. "There goes the third one." He lowered his arm. "Now, watch."

The three horsemen raced away northward, still keeping the woodshed between themselves and the house. Fred flapped his arms and twisted in the seat. "Let's go, Kelly, or do you want to just set out here; they tell me gettin' sunburnt is real popular back east."

Without a word O'Bryon leaned to unwind his lines and kick off the brakes. His big horses understood what was required of them before he flipped the lines and leaned to start the wagon moving. Walt eased back down and Fred, looking down from the seat, asked if he was bleeding. When Walt shook his head, Tower continued to lean, looking down for a moment or two, then grunted and straightened around. It was hot, but until this moment it had not occurred to Fred Tower some of the reason for his discomfort was that he was still wearing the old coat he'd had on when he and O'Bryon had first driven into the settler's yard not very long after sunup.

He shed the coat, rolled up his sleeves, loosened his collar, and reset his old hat. The big sorrel rumps moving in front of him in alternating unison held his attention until half the distance had been covered. Then he leaned back and spoke quietly to O'Bryon, his gaze narrow, his tone philosophical. "Y'know, Kelly, years back when I drove the camp-wagon for a cow outfit day in and day out it come to me that unless a man got out in front of horses, his view would always be the same."

O'Bryon neither looked around nor commented. Flat out behind and below the wagon-seat where Walt was shielding his eyes from direct sun rays, he might have smiled if he had not been preoccupied with thoughts about Elizabeth Bartlett.

He did not know all her story but was satisfied that it had seldom been pleasant because life never was for these people who tried to escape hardship somewhere else by crossing the Missouri in search of something better, and being forced to survive worse hardships before they even got out where they could dare to dream and hope. And for Elizabeth Bartlett there had been no hope for more than a year now.

He thought of the rangemen, had no doubt but that he would be able to identify them given a little time, and in an almost detached manner thought of the possible outcome if he met them again—even flat on a plank in the back of a wagon.

Kelly suddenly jerked his horses to a halt and half arose from the seat as he yelled ahead. "Friends, lady, friends. We're the same fellers was here earlier . . . We still got Constable Cutler in back . . . We don't have any guns neither."

Walt raised up and Fred Tower squinted in perplexity from the house to O'Bryon's face. Neither of them had seen the sun flash a bluish reflection off a rifle barrel from a hole in the south side of the log wall. They did not see the gun until it moved as someone inside withdrew it from the loophole.

Kelly sat down, hard, let his breath out, and eased up on the lines again. He drove almost the entire remaining distance to the rear yard before speaking again.

"Y'know, I had an aunt once who said I had the makings of a good schoolteacher." He let the lines go slack for as long as was required for him to lift his old hat, vigorously scratch his sorrel head, and drop the hat back down. "I should have listened to her. Nobody waylays schoolteachers drivin' wagons or aims guns at 'em from loopholes."

CHAPTER 10

Back to Town

ELIZABETH BARTLETT did not come out until Fred and Kelly had rigged a blanket above Walt to shade him, and even then she came no farther than the rear doorway, and she was cradling a long-barreled Winchester rifle in her arms as she looked toward the wagon from a gray, haggard face.

Walt wanted to raise up but they had tied the old blanket on a slanting angle which made it impossible for him to see the back of the house. He might have protested as they were approaching the house but kept silent because he doubted that they would turn back.

He heard their boots on the slabwood of the tiny porch, and afterward there was no sound at all for a very long time.

They came heavily back out of the house, walked around to the open side of the wagon, and stood solemnly gazing at the constable. Walt met their eyes. "Dead?"

"Yeah," Fred said softly. "He's dead. I never saw a person that wasted and wrung out. The bones are stickin' up against the skin."

"How is she?" Walt asked.

O'Bryon replied, "Ready to drop. The house smells awful, not just from burnt gunpowder neither. Worse than a tan yard."

"Bring her outside," Walt said.

Tower and O'Bryon stood looking back at Cutler without speaking for a long time, then Kelly straightened up a little. They trooped back to the house like squaw Indians, one behind the other, and Walt propped himself high enough to pull the shading blanket loose. He was watching the door when she emerged and he was shocked at her appearance. She had left the rifle behind, her red-coppery hair was dull to match the expression in her sunken eyes. She moved listlessly as she came around the wagon with her escort and stopped to gaze in at Constable Cutler. She said, "My husband died," in a toneless voice. "I . . . I was just sitting there at the table. I didn't hear them—maybe I did but wasn't conscious of hearing them. A man riding a bay horse rode up to the porch and without yelling that they were out there or saying anything at all, fired through the door."

Walt looked past where Kelly and Fred were listening. He said, "We'll take you to town and you can—"

"No," she said with a little force. "No."

Walt looked back at his friends again. Neither of them made a sound. He got up a little higher against the sideboard. She watched him do this with a flicker of the earlier concern appearing in her eyes. "You should be lying flat, Constable. The doctor said . . ."

She collapsed very slowly, like someone whose legs had simply lost their ability to support any weight. Kelly caught her and Fred breathed a startled and concerned mild oath.

O'Bryon held her, looking at Walt as though waiting to be told what to do. Walt motioned toward the tailgate. "Put her in here with me and we'll take her to town. She couldn't stay out here anyway."

O'Bryon nodded, then said, "What about him, in the house?"

Tower was already freeing the tailgate to lower it. "He'll still be here if we come back to dig a grave, Kelly. He's not goin' anywhere. I'll help you boost her up here."

They had little difficulty even though the unconscious woman was inert and difficult to control as they tried as gently as possible to get her settled atop the straw. Walt raised the blanket to shield her wasted face from direct sunlight.

Fred was rattling tailgate chain as Kelly went over to the house, looked inside, shook his head, and closed the door. He had climbed to the wagon-seat and picked up the lines before he was able to think rationally about their situation, and as he leaned back he shot a narrow look along the distant hilltops that made a three-quarters distant circle around the Bartlett homestead in the shape of a mule-shoe. He spoke to no one in particular when he said, "They're watching," and raised his voice to talk up the big horses.

Fred's brow puckered. "Wait, I'll get that rifle from the house."

They waited. Fred came back with the rifle, a saddlegun and an old six-gun without any trace of the original bluing on it, but it was loaded, and as Fred put it on the seat between himself and Kelly, he said, "If they try that again someone is goin' to arrive early in hell."

The big horses plodded; it was hot in the neck with its surrounding low hills, there was no moving air until they got back around the south hillock starting down the same trail they had taken about an hour and a half before on their way back to the Bartlett claim. Kelly had little to do; the big horses hung their heads and walked steadily over their own earlier tracks, the trail marked as far as the place where they had been stopped by the rangemen.

Beyond that spot the team traveled by instinct the way any horses would have done with slack lines; they knew where they were going and when they got there they knew the harness would be hauled off, they would be turned out to roll, then fed. That's all they knew because it was all they had to know.

Fred suggested that they get some of the whiskey down Elizabeth Bartlett, who had been lying on her side in the straw, limp and seemingly lifeless since they had boosted her into the wagon.

At Fred's suggestion she dully responded. "Whiskey won't help. Nothing will."

They drove an hour in total silence. With Peralta's rooftops finally in sight the three men exchanged a look and Walt suggested they take her to the rooming house and get the town midwife to look after her. Kelly changed course to enter town at the north end, which was in the direction of the rooming house, and Elizabeth sat up to watch the town come out to them. The darkness under her eyes had deepened, the listless sag of her body told its tale, and Walt Cutler watched her expecting her to collapse again but she remained upright looking at the town without seeing any of it.

There were people at the upper end of town and southward, down in front of the general store upon the opposite side of the road, a number of men were leaning in overhang shade making desultory conversation. When the green spring-wagon came up onto the stageroad in full view of anyone on Main Street who happened to be looking northward, a number of people turned slowly, including the men in front of the general store.

Kelly pulled in alongside the rooming house porch, set his brakes, and got wearily down to help Fred. More people appeared down the roadway, summoned from stores by other people. No one made a move to walk northward; they simply stood and stared as Elizabeth was taken inside the rooming house. Some were beginning to drift away when Tower and O'Bryon emerged and let down the tailgate so they could climb in and push Walt on his wide plank far enough outward so he could be lifted from the wagon.

People watched in dumb astonishment as Walt was carried into the rooming house. The door had scarcely closed behind him when the onlookers scattered in all directions. They had recognized the man who had been carried inside. Gus Heinz, who had been in town since morning for supplies, walked into the bank seeking Jim McGregor.

The measure of McGregor's astonishment could have been gauged by the slowness with which he removed the cigar from his mouth, then hunched forward staring at Heinz.

Across the road and southward a hundred or so yards where the stage company had its palisaded corralyard, a slight man with elfin features rushed into the manager's office and related what he and a couple of other dozen people had just seen up at the rooming house. The manager looked exasperatedly from the brisk older man he had been arguing with to the messenger, his annoyance at being interrupted very obvious, but whatever unkind thing he was about to say died on his lips. He stared at the tale-bearer. "Constable Cutler? Are you plumb sure?"

The slight, elfin-faced man bobbed his head up and down like it was an apple on a string. "Him and a woman. Fred Tower 'n Kelly O'Bryon was with 'em. It was them carried the constable inside."

The brisk man standing there listening to this exchange said, "The woman . . . The woman will be . . ." He let it trail off as the other two men looked blankly at him. He started for the door as the stage company's local manager said, "Doctor, like I said, it'll only be an hour before the southbound stage leaves for Mineral Wells, an' our stages don't wait."

The brisk man was already through the door.

At the rooming house a barrel-shaped graying woman with a bulldog jaw and steely gray eyes tiptoed out of a room on the west side of the corridor and stared hard at Fred and Kelly as she eased the door closed without a sound at her back. She said, "What happened; she near's to being struck dumb an' out of her head. Who is she?"

O'Bryon was among Peralta's single men who resided at the rooming house. He had lived there almost seven years. He and the proprietress knew each other very well. He said, "She's the wife of a settler who lives out a ways to the northeast. Her name is—"

"I asked what happened to her," the steely-eyed graying woman said.

Kelly sighed and jerked his head toward the door nearest to him on the opposite side of the hallway. "Ask Walt . . . He got shot. I want to catch the Mineral Wells coach before it leaves at five o'clock to send word for that doctor to come back up here . . . Ask Walt, Bertha . . ." Kelly was turning away and Fred also faced the doorway. They left the burly woman looking after them. She was still watching them as they neared the door at the exact moment it was flung violently inwards, striking Fred lightly as Dr. Eaton came in. Before Kelly recovered Eaton snapped at him. "Where is the constable?"

Fred pointed toward one of the doors lining the hallway. Dr.

Eaton marked the particular door with a stare as he said, "Someone said you brought a woman into town with you." His dark gaze came back to Fred Tower. "Missus Bartlett?"

"Yes."

"Her husband . . . ?"

"Dead, Doctor," stated Fred, jerking his head in the direction of the door the burly woman was standing in front of. "She . . . Ask the constable. It's a long story . . . She was standin' beside the wagon an' her legs just let go. She passed out so we loaded her in with Walt and fetched her along to town."

Dr. Eaton pushed past. In the face of his formidable forward march the hard-eyed woman stepped aside, opened the door for him to enter first, then followed him and closed the door behind herself.

Kelly flapped his arms and looked at Fred Tower. "I need a drink," he said, and pushed past the door out into slanting sunlight. It was midafternoon with the sun on its way toward a string of heat-hazed distant mountains.

Fred veered away leaving O'Bryon to stride toward the Horseshoe Saloon alone. Fred did not especially need a drink, he simply wanted to get down to his harness store and sit down where it was cool and calm and quiet, where he could think.

The man who helped out at the store in Fred's absence wore thick glasses. He was a stringbean of an individual, tall and slightly bent and thin. He peered like an owl at Fred and had enough presence of mind not to say a word as Fred went to a rickety old chair near the cold wood-stove and sank down as though he had expended his last ounce of energy just reaching the chair.

For a long time he sat gazing out the window into the roadway, then he said, "Jake, about a week back one of us peddled some of the Messican's carved spur-leathers to a cowboy. I think it was me but I'm not sure."

The owlish-looking man leaned on the counter studying his employer. "That's right, it was you," he said quietly. "What about it?"

"I can't for the life of me recollect the man I sold them to," replied Tower, slowly bringing his gaze around.

The owlish-eyed man said, "I don't know his name, Fred, but I saw you sell them to him. He rides for the White ranch. I've seen him around town."

Tower's squint deepened. "You're sure, Jake?"

"Fred, I was standin' right over there at the cutting table. I heard you make the sale and seen him pay you and walk out with the straps. That was the only sale we made that afternoon, otherwise one of the Heinz boys come in for the Miles City saddle you put new rigging in, and O'Bryon's dayman brought in some busted halters to be patched up . . . Yes, I'm sure."

Fred made an unconscious grope for his plug and bit off a corner while gazing at his helper. He got the cud properly pouched into his cheek and returned the plug to his shirt pocket without taking his eyes off the man leaning on the counter. Then he said, "When was the last time you saw this feller, Jake?"

The answer came back after a slight delay. "Last week I think it was, down in front of the general store with some other rangeriders shootin' the bull while their supply wagon was being loaded . . . Why? What about him?"

Fred's gaze drifted back to the roadway where shadows were thickening. "I want to know his name. Better yet, are you plumb certain you'd know the son of a gun if you saw him again?"

This time the leaning man's weak eyes narrowed slightly behind their thick lenses. "Fred, what's wrong?"

Tower scowled. "I asked if you'd know him again if you saw him?"

"Yes, I'd know him . . . Now, Fred, I don't want to get into trouble."

Tower arose and shoved his hat to the back of his head. "I've had a heck of a day," he told his helper. "I'm goin' into the back room and lie down for a spell . . . Hand me that bottle of Old Crow from under the counter, will you? . . . Thanks . . . Jake, I'm not going to get you into any trouble, I just want you to point that man out to me . . . See you in the morning. Lock up, will you?''

· Jake agreed to lock up but as he watched Fred disappear into the storeroom where there was an old army cot, his watery pale eyes behind their thick glasses did not reflect a conviction that Fred would not get him into trouble.

CHAPTER 11

Toward Sundown

DR. EATON missed the late-day coach and when the stage company's local manager saw Eaton hunched at the café counter talking spiritedly to a pair of men he recognized as Fred Tower and Kelly O'Bryon, the stage company's man turned on his heel heading up to the Horseshoe. He did not want to have to confront that confounded pill pusher who had already argued with him once today, and with each five-cent glass of beer at the Horseshoe a drinker was entitled to eat at the free food counter.

Fred had slept. He had arisen still dog-tired and had both bathed and shaved, and as though through a miracle, those things had refreshed him. Kelly O'Bryon had not gone to those extremes but he had slept. When he arose he was ravenous and he still was although he had eaten half his meal while Dr. Eaton talked.

Eaton could not believe his two companions at the café counter had been so irresponsible and thoughtless as to submit the constable to all the abuse they had compelled him to endure in his poor physical condition.

Kelly went on eating. Fred sipped black coffee, staring straight ahead at some flies walking on the inverted glass bowl atop the pie-plate, trying to find a way inside.

When Dr. Eaton, who was an irascible, birdlike individual, had finally started to get on Fred's nerves he put down the coffee and said, "What did the constable tell you about today?"

Eaton's quick, penetrating dark eyes sprang to Tower's face. "That Bartlett died and you three brought his widow to town . . . And that there was some unpleasantness and you two put the team-horses into a run . . . I'll tell you, gents, except that the constable's got the constitution of a horse you probably would have killed him today."

Kelly threw back his head, emptied half a cup of java straight down, then shoved the cup aside and reached for his eating implements again.

Fred studied the frustrated flies for a moment, then said, "Doctor, did you figure to head for Mineral Wells today?"

"Yes, and as luck would have it I broke a front wheel coming into town and the blacksmith can't fix it until tomorrow. Otherwise I would have been well on my way . . . Why did you ask?"

"Well," Fred said laconically, fishing for his plug, "maybe it's providence." He left that hanging in the air with Dr. Eaton gazing perplexedly at him until he had the cud pouched into his cheek, then he went on speaking in his customary unhurried manner. "Maybe it'd pay you to hang around town tomorrow. I got a feelin' there's goin' to be need of your services." Fred faced Eaton and smiled, arose, spilled silver coins atop the counter, and walked out of the café.

Dr. Eaton looked to his left where Kelly O'Bryon was finally beginning to ease up. "Did you hear that?" Eaton asked, and Kelly nodded while reaching for the coffee cup to empty it.

"What did he mean?" the doctor inquired.

Kelly rinsed his mouth with coffee, put the cup down, and turned green eyes upon the medical man. "I think he meant somebody's goin' to get hurt tomorrow, maybe even killed," and as Dr. Eaton's dark eyes brightened upon O'Bryon, the liveryman held up one hand. "I'm guessing, Doctor, but I can tell you for a fact three men come within an ace of murderin' the constable today." Kelly rocked a couple of time before hoisting himself upright. While he was fishing for coins he said, "How is the lady, Doctor?"

Eaton did not reply at once. He waited until O'Bryon had put down the coins beside his empty plate, then he said, "The constable didn't tell me anything about such an encounter."

Kelly nodded his head looking thoughtfully at the medical

man. "He was dead tired, wasn't he? Anyway, maybe he didn't want to tell you—or anyone else for that matter."

Kelly also departed leaving Dr. Eaton gazing at the platter of food he had scarcely touched. The cafeman came shuffling along in his bedroom slippers—about all he could stand on his feet since freezing them nine years earlier—and halted. The cafeman was pretty much running to lard now, but years earlier he had been a compactly powerful man with a truculent disposition and had scars to prove it. He looked at the platter, looked at Dr. Eaton, and made a great show of leaning down upon his counter with his face about eighteen inches from Dr. Eaton's face, small gray eyes like wet stones.

"Mister," he said, "when a body stands over a hot stove on a hot day to cook a decent meal, he expects folks to eat it. Otherwise what in hell do they come into a café for?"

Dr. Eaton returned the cafeman's steady gaze, and reddened. In a testy voice he said, "Mister, there is a badly wounded man up at the rooming house—your town constable. And there is an ill and exhausted settler-woman up there whose husband died today. All the heart's gone out of her. Did you ever see a whipped dog? She doesn't want to live." Eaton paused to look at his untouched meal. "If you didn't spend all your time over that hot stove you'd know what's happening in your town."

Eaton arose and stood stiffly counting out coins under the gaze of the disagreeable cafeman. When he put the silver on the counter he also said, "There's nothing wrong with the food. But not all of us think with our bellies. Some of us do it with our hearts. Good day."

The cafeman continued to lean atop the counter watching Dr. Eaton hike briskly across the roadway and step up on the far side, turn north, and continue his march in the direction of the rooming house.

The cafeman sighed, picked up the scarcely touched meal, and padded back into his cooking area to salvage what had not been touched; it would soon be suppertime and the single men would be drifting in from such places as the blacksmith shop and the corralyard to be fed. It never hurt to have a little grub handy that could be heated up again.

The barrel-shaped graying woman met Dr. Eaton at the rooming house door and held it for him to enter. She spoke in a lowered voice. "She's still sleeping. What was in that pink stuff you made her drink?"

Eaton's dark eyes still showed smouldering fire from his encounter with the cafeman. "I told you it was to make her sleep."

"This long, Doctor?"

Eaton's color climbed a little. "Perhaps," he said icily, "you would like to take over my doctoring trade."

The graying woman's steely gaze hardened a little. "I'm worried about her."

"And what do you think I am, madam? All you know is what you've seen since she arrived here. I was at their log shack today. I know more than you do about what caused her to become a vegetable . . . I was supposed to be in Mineral Springs by tomorrow morning . . . I'll need a room for the night and maybe for tomorrow as well."

The graying woman nodded her head and softened her gaze a little. Dr. Eaton began feeling ashamed of himself so he too eased up a little. "Bertha, is it?"

"Yes. Bertha Maloney."

"Bertha, if you want to help her, then sit with her. That medicine will wear off in another hour or so. She'll need someone, preferably another woman. Sit with her. I don't think she'll want to talk but if she does, listen to her. Be very kind to her—and if you have some hot broth . . . I'll be in the constable's room."

Dr. Eaton marched down the hall and entered Constable Cutler's room without knocking. It was on the west side of the building and had a window but someone had pulled a blanket across to keep light out, so about all Dr. Eaton could make out was a white face on an old pillow looking at him as he crossed to the window and yanked the blanket aside, then turned.

The room was still dingy, mostly as a result of sunset having come and gone. He lighted a coal oil lamp, set it firmly on a small table near the bed, and pulled a chair around to sit on before he said, "Well, how do you feel now, after being bathed and re-bandaged?"

Walt had been sleeping. He raised a hand to his stubbly cheeks before replying, "Like someone who has been yanked through a knothole. How is Missus Bartlett?"

Eaton's expression reflected brief annoyance. "Let's talk about you. I can't explain why you didn't bleed more."

"Not enough left to trickle out," said Walt.

"Nonsense, Constable," stated the doctor, and cleared his throat. "You have an extraordinary constitution . . . Who tried to murder you today?"

Walt stifled a yawn. He was comfortable, totally relaxed, and whatever the pink liquid was Dr. Eaton had dosed him with earlier, its residual effect after several hours of sleep was a sensation of very pleasant lassitude. His mind was clear but his body felt too weak to punch its way out of a paper sack.

"I don't know who tried to murder me today, Doctor. He had a rag over his face."

"Why, Constable? Would it have been the same man who bushwhacked you?"

Walt pondered his reply. Probably by now everyone in town knew at least the high points of what had happened to him, and for all he knew they might also have some ideas about what else had happened. Still, for a short while before the doctor had walked in, he had been thinking, and at this particular moment he was not feeling in a mood for volunteering information, so eventually he said, "Your guess is as good as mine about the bushwhacker. About the rest of it—I don't have it sorted out yet." Walt then brought up a topic he was sure would get the medical practitioner off nosy questions. He said, "I think I'll be fit to drive a buggy in a day or so. I feel a lot—"

Eaton exploded. "You are an absolute idiot! Talking to you is like talking to a stone wall! All right! All right, Constable, get out of that bed in a day or two and kill yourself. What good does it do for me to work myself to a frazzle trying to keep people like you alive?" The doctor abruptly stood up, very stiffly, and glared. "You think because some kindly but misguided spirit rode in that wagon with you today that you are indestructible? Let me tell you: Today you were lucky. That's all there was to it." Eaton marched to the door and yanked it open as he fired his parting salvo. "If you leave that bed short of two weeks I will not be responsible for you!"

He slammed the door after himself.

Walt's face remained expressionless as he regarded the closed door. He had deliberately got Eaton away from topics Walt preferred not to discuss, but he had not thought Eaton would become as furious as he had; perhaps the doctor from Mineral Wells had had a bad day. In any case, the questions he had wanted to ask about Elizabeth Bartlett were not now going to be answered.

He considered the coal oil lamp. It was too far away for him to reach so he closed his eyes with his head turned from the light, and again the door opened. This time it was the graying woman who owned the rooming house. She had a bowl of something that smelled of cooked chicken, which it was, but there was no meat, just broth.

Walt's stomach responded instantly although he'd had no appetite until now. She approached the bed looking down at his face, and she smiled, which was something she did not do easily.

He watched her drag a chair to his bedside as she said, "You'd think I was runnin' a hospital. Lucky I only have three overnighters today . . . Open your mouth."

She spooned hot chicken broth into Walt in the manner of a mother bird feeding a fledgling, and frowned in concentration as she did this, lips pursed in a straight line.

He ate every drop from the bowl and she leaned back frowning at him. "I'll get more," she said. "I didn't expect you'd eat this well."

He stopped her with a question. "How is Missus Bartlett?"

The burly older woman settled upon the chair holding the bowl and gazing past Walt at the gloomy wall for a moment before answering. "I don't know. I been through my share . . . but I expect she's been through just as much, maybe more, an' all in a very short while. The doctor gave her some medicine to sleep and it worked real good. The problem is, Constable, some time she had to wake up an' nothing was changed when she did." Her steely eyes came gently back to his face. "I just plain don't know how she is. Physically, all right I guess. I bathed her and there wasn't no bruises or anything like that . . . It's in her head. What can you do about something like that?"

He told her about Elizabeth Bartlett's husband. That seemed to strike a responsive chord in the older woman because she spoke with bitterness in her voice when he had finished. "I been a widow fifteen, goin' onto sixteen years. I've had time to think about it; seems to me some women are born to be early widows. Why, I got no idea—they just seem to be." She regarded him with all the hardness gone from her eyes. "I'll set with her tonight. She wouldn't eat earlier but maybe along toward morning she will." The soft gray gaze lingered on Cutler. "When I was washin' her she said something about men attacking her shack with guns . . . Is that what happened or was she just out of her head?"

"It happened."

"Why? Who were they? . . . Well, all right, I can see in your face I shouldn't have asked that." The graying woman arose heavily and paused to look at Constable Cutler in the bed. "You want more broth? I made a big potful."

He smiled at her. "It's the best chicken broth I ever ate."

She smiled back. "I guess that means you want more. My Lester was real partial to my chicken broth. I've seen that man set at the kitchen table and eat four bowls of it one right after the other."

"Maybe you could look in on the settler-lady on your way back," Walt said.

The woman nodded. "I figured to anyway . . . She looks like a warmed-over dead person. Never moves, just lies there lookin' at the ceiling . . . Constable, what would you think if I was to put a little whiskey into some broth for her?"

Walt's eyes twinkled. "I think that'd do her a world of good—if you could get it down her."

The graying woman reached the door looking very determined. "I'll get it down her," she said and left the room.

CHAPTER 12

Fitting Pieces Together

AN hour after his second bowl of chicken broth, when Constable Cutler was somewhere between sleeping and not sleeping, a heavy fist rattled his door and because of the utter silence it startled him into full wakefulness.

His visitor this time was Gus Heinz, the squarely built, pale-eyed cowman from north and east of town, and he neither smiled nor spoke as his shrewd small eyes took in the constable's coloring and expression. He merely nodded, advanced upon the only chair in the room, nodded as he sat down, then glanced annoyedly at the coal oil lamp, which was smoking. He arose, went over to adjust the wick, and returned to the chair. This time as he sat down he said, "I've seen better-lookin' meat hangin' on a hook." He glanced at his work-thickened, scarred hands and also said, "I need someone to put some pieces of a puzzle into place for me." This time when the pale blue eyes came up they were piercing. "Walt, how long was you out there at that homestead?"

Cutler answered shortly. "A couple of days after I was shot. Why?"

Heinz looked at his hands again. "My boys was north of that neck of land couple of days ago. They sat their horses in some trees and watched a solitary horseman skirt along the eastern hill out there, only he was stayin' down the far side just out of sight from anyone down in the neck, and he was ridin' with a Winchester across his lap—not a carbine, a rifle." Heinz paused and raised his eyes again. "They figured he was after antelope or maybe deer and after he passed down along that hill southward, they turned off and forgot about him. When they come home they told me about him at supper. It didn't mean anything to us; there's lots of pothunters out this time of year. Then this evenin' Jim McGregor said you'd been out there somewhere and had got shot. He told me to go see Fred or Mike. I talked to Mike."

Heinz straightened up. "The question I want to ask is this: Ron Sexton who rides for White ranch got killed not very far from where my sons saw that feller with the rifle, and a couple of White rangemen talked to a young feller who's been ridin' for us this year an' he said they'd heard talk that no homesteader could do something like that and get away with it." Heinz drew a breath. "Walt, could you identify that bushwhacker?"

"No. He was too far away, Gus, but your boys cleared up one thing for me: I believe he was a good shot, but I thought he'd most likely used a carbine. With a rifle and good sights he'd still have to be a good shot, but there are lots of men who could have done as well and a few who could have been better using a rifle."

Heinz looked disappointed. He flung a thick arm over the back of the chair and ranged a disinterested look around the room, then back again. "Are you up to another question?" he asked.

Walt nodded.

"Did you have any idea White ranch has been losing cattle?"

Walt's eyes widened a little. He and the cowman looked steadily at one another. "No, I didn't have, Gus. Are they?"

Heinz raised and lowered his head one time and continued to sit with his arm over the back of the chair as he solemnly studied the man in the bed. "Yeah. Maybe not many. The day their boss left for the east they made a decent gather. The next day, hours before sunup, they commenced a drive . . . North, Walt, not south toward Mineral Springs."

"How do you know that, Gus?"

"I was out with my boys and the crew. We had the wagon and expected to be at the marking ground for maybe three, four days. It's a long drive so we left the yard about three in the morning . . . Maybe five, six miles out we could hear cattle bawling in the dark. Now then, if you know anything about cattle, Walt, they don't a whole herd of them bawl in the dark and keep it up unless there's a bear, maybe some wolves, among them, or they're being driven . . . I left the wagon and went to see." Heinz withdrew his arm from the back of the chair. "Yeah, I can guess what you're thinking; that they own miles of range to the north and was driving cattle to better grass."

Walt said, "And . . . ?"

"They already took most of their wet cows up there three weeks ago. There's not that much feed. If it was all eaten down they'd have to bring their cattle close to the home-place, which they would not do because then they'd be using up the winter grass they figure to get through on. They've never done anything like this since I've known the outfit, and that is a long time."

Walt said, "But that don't mean someone is stealing cattle, Gus."

Heinz lifted a long upper lip in a humorless grin. "It does, Walt, if they drive those cattle plumb out of the country, over the hills, and hand them over to some fellers who was waiting and those fellers continued pushing them north."

"Gus, maybe Mr. White made a private sale with someone. Maybe he authorized that drive."

Heinz made that bleak grin again, small blue eyes fixed on the constable. "Maybe, Walt, maybe." He arose and stood in front of the chair. "One more thing, partner: You know old Bellingham who works for Kelly O'Bryon?"

"Yeah. Not well but I know who he is."

"He lost three or four horses out of a corral yesterday while Kelly was gone, and went after them hoping to catch 'em before Kelly found out what'd happened and maybe fired him . . . He cornered the horses and got shanks on 'em in among some pine trees in the direction of that homesteader's place. He head-and-tailed them and struck out back for town but aimed due east through the timber for the stageroad . . . He saw three riders skulkin' down toward a spit of trees with guns in their laps. A long ways off he saw a wagon coming. He said it was so far off he couldn't more than just make it out . . . Maybe, and maybe he had a bottle with him. Anyway, when he got the horses back he kept quiet because if he'd told Kelly he'd been out there Kelly would have demanded to know why. You see?"

"Yeah, I see."

"Well, Walt. He recognized one of those three riders who was coming down through the timber as he was passing eastward . . . Mike Kelso." Heinz gazed without blinking at Walt Cutler. "The same son of a gun I watched heading up that northward drive of old man White's cattle."

Walt had a question for the cowman. "What did he see those three men do?"

"Nothing. They rode down into a spit of pines and stopped there. He kept moving and didn't see them again. But what he wouldn't tell Kelly he told me because I bought him a bottle; it was Mack for a fact and maybe a couple of his riders. Walt, they was riding with guns across their laps on the south side of that hill which borders the homesteader's place. And there was a fight out there today, wasn't there?"

"Yeah, there was a fight."

Heinz flapped thick arms and regarded the lawman in silence. Walt eased his head back deeper into the pillow and stared at the closed door of the room for a long time, then said, "I guess everyone knows there was a fight out there, eh?"

"Maybe not everybody," Gus replied, "but the story is goin' the rounds. By tomorrow everyone ought to know . . . Walt, just tell me one thing: Why did that ambusher shoot you?"

"Because from that far off he probably thought I was the settler and if Sexton had friends like that . . ."

"Did the settler kill Sexton?"

"No, Gus, he couldn't have. He couldn't even get out of bed. He died sometime last night or early this morning. He had lung fever."

"Then who did kill Sexton?"

Walt looked up at the older man. "I don't have any idea."

Gus Heinz stood slumped in thought for a moment before speaking again. "All right, pardner. Get well. I think you're into me for about three dollars at the card room an' I want a chance to get it back." Heinz went slowly to the door, still pondering, and turned as he reached for the latch. "I'm goin' to find out where those cattle went," he said, and left the room.

The lamp was guttering and smoking. Outside it was dark with an opaque cast from the moonlight and starshine, and if Walt'd had some idea of getting a good night's rest before Gus Heinz had come calling, he had no such idea afterwards.

He groaned to himself. He'd never cared much for the White ranch rangeboss, but he would never have considered Kelso a rustler. As for the rest of what Heinz had told him, he knew most of it had to be true because it fit in with what he knew and had not told Heinz.

He wanted to talk to the old hostler down at O'Bryon's barn. Not because he had doubts but because he thought old Bellingham might remember more than he'd told Gus in exchange for a bottle of whiskey.

And finally: Who did kill the man named Sexton who rode for the White cow outfit?

It was turning chilly so he snugged up the covers. That was the last thing he remembered until sunlight was being reflected off some buildings behind the rooming house and coming past the pulled-back blanket over the window.

Bertha Maloney poked her head in and peered at him. He smiled; he knew he looked like the wrath of God but he didn't feel like it so he said, "Is any of the meat left you made that broth out of?"

She continued to lean in the doorway gazing at him. "I was up all night," she replied flatly.

He remembered that and said, "I'm not really hungry."

"You don't lie very well, Constable. I'll fetch you something after a while." She did not withdraw her head from the doorway. "Can you walk?"

He thought he knew what she had in mind and got red in the face. "Sure I can walk," he retorted, not sure whether he could or not.

"Then you go across the hall and set with Missus Bartlett

until I feed the boarders and have time to bring something for the pair of you." She withdrew and closed the door.

Walt was on the verge of asking why she thought he ought to do this when the door closed.

At the first wary shift of his legs he knew he could not walk. He did not move his legs again; the pain he had not felt since yesterday had returned and did not depart for about an hour.

He could put both hands under his head without discomfort, and he could tell by the sounds his stomach was making that it was still functioning independently of his wounds.

His face itched; it was covered with more beard stubble than he'd ever had before. He scratched and listened to muted sounds coming from beyond the door, wondered how he was going to accomplish anything while flat on his back and was feeling peevish when the door opened and Dr. Eaton looked in, freshly shaved, clean and annoyingly fit as he walked to the edge of the bed.

Walt rolled his eyes upwards. "Well, I'm not dead," he said sourly.

"I didn't expect you to be, Constable, and you're not going to be—in spite of yourself—because I had a long, serious talk with the liveryman and he will not let you have a rig if you promise to sign over your wages for a year. So you're not going out of town after all. Now keep your arms up under your head like that and let me have a look at you."

Walt stared at the top of the door as he said, "How is the lady across the hall?"

Dr. Eaton, lips pursed, eyes intent, acted as though he had not heard the question, and Walt would not have repeated it if the alternative was being dragged behind wild horses.

But, when the re-dressing and re-bandaging were completed, Dr. Eaton went to the chair and sat down facing the bed. "If you break a leg I can make you as good as new. If you catch the measles I can take care of that, and even if you have a man-killing headache from drinking all night I can make you feel human again. Even bullet wounds . . ." He relaxed in the chair. "For what happens inside your head no medical man alive can do much about. If you're hopelessly insane, why then we can certify you into an asylum . . . For Missus Bartlett there is absolutely nothing I can do, Constable. God knows I wish there was something. I can make her sleep but it's all waiting there when she wakes up."

Walt raised his eyes to the top of the door again. He had seen shock and grief before but never as the handsome woman across the hall had experienced it.

The doctor was on his feet. "I asked the landlady to bring her over here to your room." At Walt's level stare the doctor shrugged. "The two of you shared a lot. And she doesn't know anyone else in Peralta. The landlady told me that. Constable, you can't do much, I know, but at least she knows you, went through a horror with you, looked after you, and what I hope may happen is that she will be a little worried about your condition." Dr. Eaton considered the window and its reflection of sunlight. For a while he was silent and when he spoke again his voice was very soft.

"Constable, I have seen people who never recovered from what this woman has gone through. Never." He turned away.

A half hour later Bertha Maloney brought two trays, set them up, and without so much as looking at the wondering man in the bed, left the room. Walt could have counted the minutes; he would not have wagered a thin dime either way that Bertha Maloney could, or could not, induce Elizabeth Bartlett to come into his room.

It seemed that an awfully long period of time had passed since the trays had been set up. So long a time in fact that Walt was sure Elizabeth would not come.

Then the door opened and Elizabeth was in the opening looking straight at him, with Bertha Maloney directly behind her giving gentle little shoves because she had a hot coffeepot in one hand.

He groped for something to say and found nothing so he just smiled a little. Elizabeth continued to look at his face as she came closer to the bed. He tried to find a spark of interest, of concern, of compassion, and all he saw was that same unseeing blankness in her eyes he had seen in them yesterday.

CHAPTER 13

A Revelation and a Shock

ROUGH, matter-of-fact, and no-nonsense Bertha Maloney got Elizabeth seated with a little table in front of her upon which was her breakfast tray. She positioned Walt Cutler with a pillow behind him and the tray on his lap, then left them, and, what neither of them could know, after closing the door Bertha hung a "Do Not Disturb" sign on the door, then went back to her kitchen.

Walt tasted the coffee and was agreeably surprised. "Fresh," he said to Elizabeth, and sipped a little more. "One thing a single man don't ever get much of is fresh java."

She sat with her hands in her lap watching him drink the coffee, seemingly detached.

He was hungry. There were eggs and buttered toast and what he assumed was orange marmalade. He looked from the food to Elizabeth. "We ought to eat," he said.

She had noticed that there were times when he reminded her of a little boy. This was one of those times. He was hungry and wanted to eat but did not want to do so in front of her unless she would also eat. She reached for the coffee cup, and, as though this were a signal, Walt attacked his breakfast.

He paused to glance in her direction. "Do you know Gus Heinz?"

She didn't. "No."

"He's a cowman. His sons saw the man who shot me, but from a distance."

She said nothing.

Walt finished the toast before speaking again. "Did you get a look at those men who attacked your house yesterday?"

"No . . . just once, after they fired into the door then rode to the woodshed to put up their horses. One of them was looking back. I'd never seen him before."

"But you'd know him if you saw him again?"

She nodded. "I'd know him again as long as I live." She considered the toast on her plate. "Those other two men with you yesterday, Constable—I am very grateful for all they did and for all you did."

He made a wry smile. "I didn't do much. There's not much a person can do flat on his back in a wagon-bed . . . They're good men, Missus Bartlett. There are a lot of good men in the Peralta country."

"Not where homesteaders are concerned, Constable."

"Yes, even where homesteaders are concerned. But it takes time, and you have to let them get used to having you in the country." He grinned. "Sound like a preacher, don't I?"

She picked up a piece of toast. "No, you sound experienced, which Henry and I weren't." She ate toast while he finished off the eggs, then she said, "I'm glad Henry never knew the cattlemen hated us so much they would try to kill us."

Walt drained his coffee cup before speaking again. "That's not why someone went after you folks yesterday. It wasn't cattlemen after settlers, it was some friends of that man who got killed up near the willow-spring on your place; they wanted revenge for that killing."

She had finished a piece of toast and was eyeing the eggs as she offhandedly said, "They thought my husband killed that man, didn't they?"

"Yes, but of course he couldn't—"

She picked up a fork as she cut across the constable's words. "I killed that man, Mr. Cutler."

Walt's eyes were fixed on her as she sliced egg with a fork and did not meet his gaze. She ate for a moment, then put down the fork and raised her face. "He had our foundered horse on a rope and rode up behind me. I was up at the spring—just sitting there—feeling my world turning to dust and crying. I didn't hear the horses until he was fairly close, but he had seen me and said our horse had been over on White range. He said he'd brought it back this time but next time they would not return it. Then he took his rope off and hit our horse as hard as he could with his rope . . . Constable, I can't explain this part very well. It had never happened to me before. Since then I've wondered if when someone is—so desolate—they aren't capable of feeling pain even when their own bodies are not being struck. I'm not making sense, am I? Well, when he hit our crippled horse it felt exactly as though he had hit me. The pain was terrible . . . I don't remember picking up the rock but I do remember springing to my feet facing him. He was coiling his rope. He had a look of total contempt on his face . . . I think I yelled or made a noise . . . Anyway he turned and I threw the rock with all my strength."

For ten seconds the silence was so complete Walt could hear his heart beating. She was looking in his direction but past him. Walt looked at the tray and slowly lifted it to set it aside. Outside a bird broke into raucous song somewhere.

Walt let his breath out slowly and pulled in another deep breath. To himself he said, "Oh hell," and looked at her. Now, she met his gaze with a fatalistic expression and said, "It was my fault you got shot. All of the trouble was my fault. Constable, I've been living with death for a year; every morning when I'd wash my husband I saw it in his face. Every night when I tried to sleep . . ." She clasped both hands in her lap without force. "When I looked at Henry that last morning I couldn't even cry. I could just sit at the table—and hurt. But I was glad for Henry. Wherever he is now is better than his life was here."

Walt was listening. He heard every word but through a sinking sensation. He rallied after a while, then he felt anger. Why had she told him about Sexton? If she hadn't, since only she and Sexton had been at the willow-spring, no one would ever have known she had killed him. Unresolved killings were a dime a dozen.

He leaned back looking at her. "Listen to me," he said quietly. "Don't ever—*ever*—say that again. Not to anyone."

Her eyes lingered on his face. She seemed to be either ordering her thoughts or framing a reply. He did not give her an opportunity to speak. "Elizabeth, your husband is gone and nothing will change that. Your hardship and suffering out there at the neck can't influence the future—whatever you do from now on. You can't live with yesterdays and that includes what happened at the willow-spring. You're young; you can no more cry for your husband for the next forty years than you can go back to the willow-spring. Are you listening?"

She was. "There is something I didn't tell you, Constable. Mixed with the hurt was relief. Henry was free of pain and I was free of watching him die. It was a great relief. . . As for that man at the spring, I know I wouldn't have reacted the way I did except for the other—thing. I wouldn't have reacted as I did even then if he hadn't struck our horse and been so contemptuously menacing . . . I don't really regret what I did up there. I probably should regret it but I honestly don't. That man represented everything in this country that is against homesteaders."

Walt felt the need for a smoke. There had been a sack of tobacco and some wheatstraw papers in his shirt pocket but he had no idea where his clothes were; they were not in the room.

Elizabeth said, "I won't—I can't—think back. A year-long nightmare."

He nodded without looking at her, and someone walking heavily down the hallway in the direction of the roadway door made the flooring groan. She stood up facing him. "It takes time, Constable. Maybe quite a bit of time. I don't suppose a person knows this much about themselves until they have to go through it, do they?" She went over beside the bed and took his tray back to the chair she had vacated as though she had thought he might upset it on the bed.

Then she left him.

The bird was still singing beyond the window and there were other sounds coming in from the town which may have been there all the time though he had not been aware of them before.

He had dredged up all his personal resources to help her, to give unstintingly of his strength, and now he was lying back feeling more troubled and drained than she had seemed to be when she had walked out of his room.

He closed his eyes. When he opened them again the bird was no longer singing and Fred Tower was sitting patiently on the chair Elizabeth Bartlett had sat on last. Fred said, "I tried to be quiet . . . You don't look as good as you did yesterday, Walt . . . I got a pony of brandy in my pocket . . ."

Walt considered the lanky older man. "Have you talked to Gus Heinz?"

Fred blinked. "Gus? No. I saw him around town but we never talked. Why?"

"Is he still in town?"

"Well, yes, I think so. He was down at the blacksmith's shop a while ago."

"Fred, go hunt him up and ask him to tell you what he told me about Mack Kelso and some of the other men who ride for him."

Fred looked blankly at his friend. "You mean right now?"

"Yeah, right now. And do me a favor; hunt up that old scarecrow who works for Kelly and tell him I want to see him up here in this room. Maybe he won't want to come . . ."

Fred Tower arose slowly, looking mildly baffled. "Bellingham is his name. All right. He'll come because I'll walk him back up here . . . Walt? What's goin' on?"

"Gus can tell you."

Tower had to be content with that since obviously Constable Cutler was not in the mood for conversation. Fred reached the rooming house's front porch before he halted, lifted his hat, scratched, dropped the hat back down, and went southward looking in the direction of the blacksmith shop. There was no one outside but that did not mean Heinz was not down there.

Bertha Maloney entered Walt's room and shot him a quizzical look as she walked over to pick up the breakfast trays. "You must be Irish," she said, and at his raised eyebrows she gave her head a little exasperated wag. "My husband was Irish an' he could charm a bird down out of a tree; he had a way with words, he did." With her features softening in recollection of her dead mate she stood holding the plates without looking in the direction of the bed. But that moment lasted little more than seconds, then she became no-nonsense Bertha again. "Dr. Eaton and I both talked to Missus Bartlett like Dutch uncles. All we got was a blank look. She was in here with you for a half an hour—and just now when I went to see how she was, she smiled at me. She even talked a little. Constable, whatever you did you sure taken a load off her shoulders."

Walt nodded in a perfunctory manner. He sure had, and he'd taken the same load onto his own shoulders. Regardless of personal feelings, of sympathy or anything else, he was an officer of the law and a woman had sat over there not two hours earlier quietly telling him she had murdered a man.

Bertha left, Walt's face itched, and when he shifted a little in the bed, there was no pain. None at all. He raised the blanket but whatever was happening under the bandages was not visible unless he wanted to poke around. He knew better than to do that as long as Dr. Eaton was likely to pop in on him at any moment.

But it was not Eaton who came into the room next, it was Fred Tower herding O'Bryon's hostler like a father driving a child towards the woodshed.

Fred stood in the doorway until old Bellingham had advanced toward the room's solitary chair, then Fred backed out and closed the door. He still had to find Gus Heinz.

Walt pointed to the chair. Bellingham sat down but did not lean back or relax as he eyed the younger man. It was anyone's guess how old Bellingham was; being a drinker he probably was not as old as he seemed, but he certainly had not been a young man for a long time.

He had watery eyes, a bloodless slit for a mouth, and a pallor beneath the sun-tanned hide of his arms and neck.

He was uncomfortable and clearly he was wary. Walt mentioned the men Bellingham had seen in the spit of pines the day before and Bellingham's wariness seemed to deepen. He may have thought this might be the reason the local lawman had wanted to see him.

He prefaced what he had to say with a request. "I'd take it right kindly if Mr. O'Bryon didn't ever know I lost four horses out of the corral when he went off and left me in charge, Constable. Could you look after that?"

Walt thought about it. If Bellingham were needed to identify the one man he had recognized in the trees, then he would have to do it publicly and Kelly would find out about the rest of it.

"I'll do everything I can, Mr. Bellingham. Kelly would understand. There never was a horseman born who didn't lose a few horses now and then. At least you got them back."

The older man had to be satisfied with that, and he may have anticipated this too because when he spoke next he looked resigned. "I saw Mack Kelso and two other riders. They came around that eastern hill behind the neck. They were just poking along like maybe they were in no hurry, and like maybe they'd been back up on the far side of that easterly hill for a spell —maybe watching the settler's place for all I know . . . And there was a wagon coming around the south hillock of the neck but it was a heck of a distance off and I didn't waste any time anyway, I wanted to get back with the horses."

"Did you know the two men with Kelso?"

"I never got a good look at them . . . Constable, when you're out, and you see three men riding through some trees with guns across their laps, you do one of two things, you hide or you ride. I rode." Bellingham's watery eyes seemed to be looking through time as he added a little more. "I been in that situation before, Mr. Cutler. Quite a few times. It don't pay to be curious."

Walt asked about the wagon but Bellingham reiterated what he had already said. "It was too far away. Maybe three, four miles. It came into sight around that south hill below the settler's place. It looked about the size of a walnut." Bellingham's eyes rested on Walt's face. "Mr. O'Bryon told me this morning it was our green spring-wagon with you on some straw in the back, but until then I had no idea about whose rig it was or anything else." The watery eyes remained on Walt. "He told me the rest of it too, about those three bushwhackers having their faces covered. Sure as I'm setting here, Constable, those were the same men I saw and the one in front ridin' a big bay horse was Mack Kelso."

CHAPTER 14

Trouble!

WHEN Fred Tower returned he had Kelly O'Bryon in tow, and clearly Fred had found Gus Heinz because as they walked into Walt's room and carefully closed the door after themselves, their faces were grave and troubled.

Walt looked at the taller, lankier man. "You saw Gus?"

Fred nodded, removed his hat, and held it in both hands. "Yeah. An' there's somethin' else. That old Studebaker wagon with the canvas top the White outfit uses for supplies and whatnot is over in front of the emporium."

Kelly O'Bryon fished out a blue bandana and mopped sweat off his face, then eyed the only chair in the room but made no move toward it. As he stuffed the handkerchief away he said, "Walt, someone's got to go out yonder and bury that Bartlett feller. In this kind of weather, and all . . ." Kelly wagged his head with unmistakable meaning.

Kelly's remark was probably appropriate but it did not strike Walt that way. He ignored Kelly to continue regarding Fred Tower. The idea which was forming in his mind was something he would never have hesitated to undertake, but the men standing near the foot of his bed were not peace officers. Nevertheless, he wanted to talk to the rangeman who had driven that Studebaker wagon into town for supplies. He saw it as his best opportunity to corral someone from the White ranch. No one would expect the supply wagon to arrive back at the ranch for the balance of the day. That would give Walt plenty of time.

If he let this chance slip through his fingers he would

probably regret it. He said, "How many men came with the Studebaker wagon, Fred?"

Tower did not know. He had seen the wagon parked in front of the general store and had recognized it, but he had not seen anyone with it.

O'Bryon had. "One," he told Cutler. "I don't know his name but I've seen him around town; sort of tall, rangy feller."

"Just one, Kelly?"

"Yeah. I was up at Fred's harness shop picking up a batch of halters Jake had repaired for me and saw the wagon come down the road and park over in front of the store. There was just one man on the seat."

Walt eyed them both. "I need a couple of deputy constables," he said, and saw understanding cross Fred's face before it came to O'Bryon.

Fred began to scowl. "Walt . . ."

"He won't have any idea, Fred. Just walk up and grab him, take away his gun. Surprise him, Fred. That's the secret of grabbing someone."

O'Bryon was staring toward the bed. He did not open his mouth for a long while, but eventually he did. "Yesterday being with you darn near got me killed and it sure as shooting got the living daylights scairt out of me. Walt, you're bad luck."

Fred approached the matter of dissent from a different perspective, and he did it in a calmer tone of voice. "I'm into my fifties," he said, speaking laconically. "I never was worth a darn with a gun, and anyway, there's a dozen younger fellers around town you could—"

"How long is that wagon going to be standing over there?" Walt asked, and because the obdurate expressions did not soften he reached to fling off the covers as though to get out of bed. Pain arrived the moment he moved his injured hip. He spoke through gritted teeth. "Help me out of here. Go ask Bertha what she did with my boots and all."

O'Bryon took several steps toward the bed and threw up an admonishing arm. "Get back in there. Are you crazy? You can't stand up let alone put your pants on. Get back down there.

Walt, for Chrissake! . . . Fred, lend me a hand. One of us has got to sit on this idiot until he starts using his head."

Tower did not move. He was standing up to his full height looking down his nose at Constable Cutler. "He's not goin' to get out of there," he stated. "All he'll do is end up in a pile on the floor . . . Come along, Kelly."

O'Bryon still had his arm outstretched as he looked over his shoulder. He thought he knew what Tower meant but wanted confirmation because he hoped his hunch was wrong. He got the confirmation. As Fred turned toward the door he said, "I'm not even plumb certain where my damned pistol is. I think it's under some old saddle-blankets in the storeroom of the shop . . . Kelly, don't stand like that, come along." Fred was holding the door open as he faced the constable. "I told that darned pill roller to hang around town today; I figured someone would need him but I sure never expected it to be me . . . All right, Walt, we'll fetch him up here, but I'm goin' to tell you right now I'm too old for this sort of thing and if he bows his neck I'm going to run."

Walt winced when O'Bryon, the last one out, slammed the door. He did not worry about them, right at that moment anyway, because he was speculating on what the rangeman might know—*if* he knew anything. If he did, then Walt was going to have him locked up and that meant when the supply wagon did not return, Mack Kelso would come looking for it—maybe—and maybe he'd send someone else.

Walt had about five hours to seize the initiative and hold it, if he could. Right at this moment he would have liked to have heard Gus relate what he knew about rustling cattle again.

It worried him that he might be jumping the gun. Except that Gus was convinced that it had been a cattle-stealing operation he had stumbled onto, Walt had nothing else to base an accusation on. But it wasn't only the rustling he wanted someone from the White ranch to explain to him. He was even more interested in the riders who had stopped the wagon and who afterwards had raced back to the Bartlett place to commit murder.

Finally, as his agitation lessened, he began to worry about

Tower and O'Bryon. If he could have known something about the man who had driven the supply wagon to town it might have helped. All he could think of at this moment was that Mack Kelso had men riding for him who would attempt to shoot their way into a settler's shack to kill someone, and they could be the same men Gus had seen stealing cattle from the ranch they worked for.

Men like that were not likely to be intimidated by one tall, rawboned older man and a shorter tobacco-chewing man —neither of whom would be wearing guns as though they wore them comfortably.

Walt Cutler was right. The rawboned rangeman who leaned on the hardware counter of the general store while a clerk checked off the supplies which had been loaded into the wagon scarcely more than glanced around when Fred and Kelly walked in from the roadway. He took back the list from the clerk and straightened up as he folded and pocketed it.

He was neither young nor old and he was sinewy and callused. He seemed likely to have some Indian blood. His face was darkly bronzed and his black eyes, which had touched upon Tower and O'Bryon moments before, gradually came fully to rest upon them as Fred walked up to within fifteen feet of the rangeman and said, "The constable wants to talk to you."

O'Bryon had his right hand lightly atop the holstered Colt he was wearing. His green eyes were fixed upon the rangeman.

When the surprise passed the cowboy dropped his arms and said, "What about?"

Fred's answer was brusque. "He'll tell you. Turn around."

The cowboy forgot about Kelly's hand and stared straight at Fred Tower. He did not turn around. He said, "I don't see no badges," and as the last word left his lips he kicked violently. Fred had seen the almost imperceptible shift of the cowboy's body weight and was twisting when the kick flashed past, caught Kelly on the left upper leg sending him sprawling.

Fred forgot about the gun stuck into the waistband of his trousers. He heard the store clerk emit a loud squawk as the cowboy stepped backwards and sideways, as light on his feet as a dancer.

Fred did not show anger, just total concentration. He went after the rangeman, hauled up just short, and as the cowboy fired a high cocked right fist, Fred slipped around it and came in with a savage strike into the cowboy's ribs.

The store clerk was squawking more loudly now and scuttling toward the back of the store.

The rangerider sagged from the rib-blow and twisted his mouth from pain, but before Fred could square around on him the cowboy was moving clear and kept on pedaling away until the pain had lessened. Then, with murder on his face, he reached for his holstered Colt.

Kelly yelled from down on one knee and simultaneously cocked his six-gun. The cowboy saw the hammer slide back, saw the barrel aimed at his middle, and raised his arms because Fred was coming after him again. He made no further attempt to draw his gun.

Fred paced himself. He had been in this identical situation a number of times in his fifty-odd years and there was one lesson he had learned very well: conserve everything, legs, arms, breath, stalk and move and wear an opponent down, never hurry.

He had been angry when he'd seen Kelly go down from that kick but he was not angry now, he was calm and deliberate. When the younger man used his better legs to dance away, Fred continued to crowd him. Neither of them threw a punch until the store owner emerged from out back with his clerk and bellowed for them to get out into the road if they wanted to fight.

While that angry roar was filling the big old room Fred ducked low, jumped ahead, jumped back to let a furious swing whistle past, and caught the cowboy with his feet tangled. He hit him over the heart, shifted, and struck him in the same side he'd injured earlier. He was coming up in front aiming for the face when the cowboy kicked with all his strength, catching Fred on a kneecap. Pain filled him as he was going down.

The rangerider who could no longer balance on his toes took two forward steps and aimed his next kick at Fred's head. Kelly hit him in the back like a catapult. The cowboy went headlong across Fred, who was rolling in an attempt to escape the kick he knew was coming.

Fred had half the breath knocked out of him when the rangeman came down atop him, but he reacted before the younger man could, reaching with fingers of steel and wrenching the younger man over, getting one forearm across the cowboy's gullet. He locked the other hand into a fulcrum position and really did not have to exert much pressure to cut off the younger man's wind. But he increased the pressure anyway, and had to ride the wildly plunging and frantically threshing cowboy like a bucking horse until the storekeeper ran up yelling to Fred that he was killing his opponent. He lunged to break Tower's grip and Kelly O'Bryon shoved the cocked six-gun into his face from a distance of fifteen inches. The storekeeper's eyes bulged, he stopped moving, looked up into O'Bryon's face, and eased back, getting redder in the face by the second.

Fred broke his grip, rolled up to his feet, and balanced on one leg, waiting. The rangeman came up slowly and sluggishly, panting for breath with his mouth wide open.

He raised a hand to his throat looking at Fred Tower from a distance of about twelve feet. His shirt was torn, his face had dirt from the floor on it, and his breathing was loud and uneven. He started to speak but only rasping sound came out.

Fred still waited, fists cocked.

The cowboy shook his head. Fred pointed to the gun. The rangerider dropped it then turned dumbly looking for something to sit on.

Fred limped over, kicked the gun away, grabbed the cowboy, and swung him around by the shoulder. He pointed toward the doorway. "Walk, you son of a gun," he stated in a knife-edged but quiet tone of voice, and followed up the order with a rough shove.

The cowboy walked past his crushed hat, still holding his

throat. Kelly marched behind him with the cocked six-gun and as Fred leaned to retrieve his own hat the storekeeper waved a furious finger at him. "Fred Tower, what's got into you, a man your age and all. Don't you ever come into this store again until you apologize. You run off my customers and scairt the whey out of my clerk. Now you—"

"Shut up," Fred said, shaping his hat and looking straight at the storekeeper. "Get me a bottle of liniment and shut up."

The storekeeper got the liniment and slammed it down atop the counter, glaring, but he did not open his mouth. He and his clerk watched Fred Tower limp out of the store.

Kelly had already driven their rangerider across to the far side of the road under the astonished stare of a dozen or so pedestrians. He halted over there to wait for Fred. When they were together driving their rangeman in the direction of the rooming house, Fred said, "How's your hip?"

Kelly was not limping. "All right. He spun me, didn't catch me full on. What kind of a son of a gun mule-kicks in a fight?"

Fred mopped sweat off his face before replying. "That kind of a son of a gun." He raised his voice slightly. "What's your name, cowboy?"

The answer was a croak. "Sackett. Frank Sackett."

"Who do you work for?"

"Mack Kelso at the White ranch."

They were nearing the sagging porch of the rooming house when Frank Sackett twisted as though to look back before speaking, and Fred reached almost lazily and slapped him with an open palm. "Save your breath, Frank. Maybe later on I'll beat the hide off you but for right now keep quiet."

There were people like statues back down the roadway on both sides, watching. A little ripple of talk erupted back down there but neither O'Bryon nor Tower looked back. One voice, deep and loud and shaking with indignation, was louder than the other voices as the furious storekeeper repeatedly exclaimed that Fred Tower must have gone out of his head; that lanky cowboy was half his age.

A man standing in the bank doorway chewing an unlighted

cigar turned to call someone inside. "Gus, come look at this. Fred and Kelly . . . Kelly's got a cocked gun in his hand. Come look. That's one of Kelso's men they got in tow."

Heinz's thick figure shouldered past the banker. He did not say a word until the trio up in front of the rooming house had disappeared inside, then he spat into roadway dust. "Mr. McGregor, I think the constable's doin' pretty well at his job for a man who can't even stand up."

McGregor looked down. "What are you talking about, Gus?"

Heinz started to walk away and did not respond.

CHAPTER 15

The Rangeman

FRED TOWER appropriated the only chair in Walt Cutler's room and sat down ignoring the others as he rolled up a trouser leg. His knee was swollen and slightly discolored. He probed it, reached for the liniment bottle in his rear pocket, and went to work, interrupting the conversation between Constable Cutler and Mack Kelso's rider as he worked on the knee.

"You're wasting time, Walt. Look at his spur leathers."

Fred dabbed on the liniment, which had a powerful smell. He did not look up. It was Kelly who spoke next. He was looking wide-eyed at the rangeman. "You're the one that dragged me."

Frank Sackett's coarse features showed fear. He refused to meet O'Bryon's stare, concentrated on looking steadily at the man in the bed. He had already told Walt his name and who he rode for, his voice harsh-sounding but less so than when he'd got off the floor down at the general store.

Walt made a point of staring at the new, hand-carved spur leathers. He let the silence drag out until Kelly broke it, then Walt raised his eyes and said, "Who was the third man, Sackett? There was you and Mack. Who was the third rider when you boys stopped the wagon because you thought it was Bartlett in back?"

Sackett's hand was at his throat. He was obviously thinking fast, and desperately. None of this was supposed to have happened; certainly not the shellacking he'd taken from that rawboned old man smelling up the room with his horse liniment.

He looked toward the window, black eyes moving like those

of a cornered animal. Walt spoke again, his voice a little harsh this time.

"You answer or they're goin' to beat it out of you."

At that statement Fred's head finally came up. He looked in disbelief at the constable. His knee was the size of a gourd and he was not sure he could even stand up let alone fight again.

Sackett shifted his weight and looked at Walt. He had in mind saying he had no idea what the constable was talking about, except for one thing: The constable knew Mack had been out there too, and that implied he knew even more, so lying might indeed result in a further beating. He said, "Sawyer Kent."

"Who is Sawyer Kent, Sackett?"

"The wrangler, horse-breaker blacksmith," croaked Frank Sackett, then spoke defensively. "Him and Ron Sexton hired on together in early spring. I think they come from Montana."

Walt eyed the rangeman. "Kent's a pretty good shot, isn't he?"

Sackett shrugged wide shoulders. "Lot of things Sawyer's good at."

"Yeah," Walt retorted dryly. "If you fellers hadn't been fools you would have ridden down to that log house . . . It wasn't the settler who killed Sexton. You'd have seen why if you'd gone down there instead of Kent trying that long shot when he hit me thinkin' I was the settler."

Sackett only picked one statement out of that discourse. His eyes were fixed on Walt. "It was the settler, it had to be him."

Walt gently wagged his head. "It wasn't . . . The settler was burning up with fever, couldn't get out of bed—and he died night before last from lung fever. Sackett, he couldn't have sat up let alone held a rifle to his shoulder."

The lanky man who looked like a 'breed let the hand drop from his throat to his side as he regarded Constable Cutler from an expressionless face, eyes as still as stones.

Walt said, "Whose idea was it to waylay the wagon with what you fellers thought would be the wounded settler in the back of it?"

Sackett did not reply for a long while. He shifted stance again and gazed in the direction of the rear-wall window. He had been hit hard with surprise and shock. There had never been any doubt but that the homesteader had killed Ron Sexton. He faced the bed again. Two things were obvious to him. The constable knew more than Sackett had expected him to know, and, from instinct, Frank Sackett knew the constable was not lying to him.

Walt repeated his question. "Whose idea was it to stop the wagon and make sure the settler got killed?"

Sackett's answer was short. "Kent."

"What about Mack, he's the rangeboss out there?"

Sackett slowly shook his head. "Yeah, he's the boss, but Kent an' Sexton . . . they had a lot to say."

"Was it Kent who led the way back to the log house after you fellers discovered it wasn't the settler in the wagon?"

"Yeah."

Walt looked at Kelly and Fred. O'Bryon was leaning on the wall and Fred had finished doctoring his knee and had rolled down the pants leg. He had been gingerly flexing the knee and seemingly paying no attention to the conversation, but when his eyes met those of Walt Cutler he said, "Something is beginnin' to clear up for me, Walt." Fred switched his attention to the rangerider. His gaze was not especially hostile, more clinically dispassionate and speculative. He was looking at Sackett but still addressing Cutler when he said, "I'd like to ask this smoked Irishman, or whatever he is, one question." Walt said nothing. Fred held the cowboy's gaze as he said, "About Sexton and this Kent feller: They was partners, right? And you think they came from Montana, right? And they had a lot to say on the ranch . . . Now then, Mr. Sackett, here is my question: Did Sexton and Kent organize a rustling operation on the White ranch?"

Sackett swallowed a couple of times before offering a protest. "All I know about is that Kent got Mack Kelso an' me to go give him cover while he settled with that homesteader for killin' his partner."

Frank slowly shook his head from side to side with his eyes fixed upon the rangeman. "Naw, Sackett. You know more'n just that. I'll tell you what I figure you know: I got no idea how Sexton an' this Kent feller ever did it, but they talked Mack Kelso into raidin' cattle off White ranch. With the owner gone you boys been busy as kittens in a box of shavings . . . Sackett, I'm not guessing. Ask the constable. We know for a fact you fellers have been stealin' cattle."

The rangeman turned to avoid Fred's unblinking stare and met Walt Cutler's equally uncompromising look. Even Kelly O'Bryon, leaning on the far wall, was staring at him. He walked over to the window, turned, and eased down upon the inside still.

Walt did not *know*—none of them actually *knew*—there was a cattle-stealing operation going on out at the White place, but Fred, who had accepted Gus Heinz's story verbatim and was not as bothered with such things as legal proof as Walt Cutler was, had sounded completely convincing because he believed what he had said.

Sackett perched over there studying the worn wooden floor. His side ached, his throat burned with a fiery dryness he had never experienced before. He had been beaten by a man twice his age and he was in the hands of the law. He was cornered.

He drew down a long breath and let it out slowly. Then he ignored Kelly and Fred as he faced the constable. "I never been in trouble with the law," he said huskily. "You let me walk out that door an' I'll tell you what I know."

Walt's reply was blunt. "You tell us what you know and then maybe we'll talk about lettin' you leave the country."

Fred pulled the old Colt from his waistband, cocked it, and aimed it. "You try to jump out that window behind you and you'll get your spine broke when I fire to stop you."

Sackett's dark skin looked paler as he stared at the gun pointing in his direction. He already knew that the lanky old man was tough as rawhide.

He looked down as he began talking. "Sexton an' Kent come south from Montana where they're wanted for cattle stealing and maybe murder; at least I overheard 'em one night talkin' about someone gettin' shot up there. When Mack hired them they was good stockmen. Him and they got real thick . . . One night the three of 'em fired a feller named Watson and took me and another feller to the barn. They said we'd all be rich before Mr. White came back; all we had to do was drive cattle over the north mountains down to a place where they had some friends waitin' to take the cattle into northern Colorado from there. It seemed likely; we had the right to move cattle anywhere on White range we wanted to, and we had no close neighbors anyway . . . We drove four herds over the mountains. Those friends of Ron's and Sawyer's paid cash on the barrelhead after a head count . . . I never had so much money before in my life. The last drive was prime steers an' a few greasy-fat dry cows."

Sackett stopped speaking but continued to look at the floor.

Walt gazed at him through an interval of silence, then said, "And when Mr. White came back . . . ?"

Sackett continued to stare at the floor, hunched on the windowsill. "I don't know."

Walt contradicted him. "Yeah, you do. You know. You were with them up to your neck. You know."

Sackett almost whispered his reply. "Kill him . . . Bury the body and keep on drivin' the cattle over the mountains until the place was cleaned out. Then we'd all head in different directions, pockets full of money."

Walt put his head down on the pillow. Kelly O'Bryon straightened up off the wall and went over by the door where there was a small table. He tested it first, then sat on it.

Fred was still holding the old cocked gun in his lap, gazing at the rangeman. He shifted the six-gun to his other hand and felt for his plug, got a chew into his cheek, repocketed the plug, and put the cocked gun back in his right hand again.

Sackett raised his head to gaze over at Constable Cutler. "Like I said, I never been in trouble with the law an' I told you the whole story. I'm ready to walk out that door."

Walt turned his head, stared at the confessed rustler, and did not bother to reply. He looked at Fred Tower. "What happened to your leg?"

"That son of a gun kicked me. He kicks as hard as a bay mule." Fred continued to sit gazing at the cowboy. "You want Kelly an' me to lock him up, Walt?"

Cutler glanced at Frank Sackett and said, "Stand up and get away from that window . . . Now then, pull up your pants legs."

As the faded trouser leg was hiked up on the right side the stitching of a knife scabbard became visible. When the entire upper part of the boot was exposed, a knife handle was visible. Kelly grunted in surprise. Walt said, "Throw that thing on the floor . . . Kelly, go around behind him and see if he's got a hide-out gun too."

Fred Tower spoke quietly to O'Bryon. "Don't cross in front of me, Kelly."

Sackett had a little nickel-plated under-and-over .44 belly-gun under his shirt in back. Kelly tossed it onto the bed and stepped away from the rangeman as he drily said, "For a feller who's never been in trouble, he's a walking arsenal."

Walt examined the little gun. It was loaded. He put a wintry look upon the rangeman as he said, "Yeah, lock him up. Take him down the back alley. It'd be better if folks didn't see you taking him to the jailhouse. And, Kelly, take the Studebaker wagon down to your barn and park it out of sight." He dropped the little gun on the covers. "One more thing you can do: There's a box of wanted dodgers in the back room of the jailhouse. I've been storing posters in there for a long time. Fetch it up here; with any luck Sackett and the others might be there."

Walt watched as Fred Tower came up off the chair on his one good leg. As Fred tested the injured leg and grimaced, Walt said, "Can you make it?"

Fred was still holding the cocked six-gun. "Yeah, I can make it. I hope this mule-kickin' rascal tries to run off down the alley." He looked at O'Bryon. "Walt, then me; I sort of resent the notion of you comin' out this scot-free, Kelly."

They yanked Sackett's belt off and used it to lash his arms

behind his back, then drove him ahead of them out into the hallway, down to the front porch, and with dusk settling, Kelly took him firmly by one arm and steered him around into the back alley.

Walt picked up the belly-gun, turned it over in his hand, then leaned to place it upon his bedside table. It had not taken the four or five hours he'd thought he might need to sweat information out of Frank Sackett, and his relief was great that Sackett had known as much as he had. If he hadn't Constable Cutler would have been in trouble up to his armpits.

He lay back to relax and think. Given the distance from town to the yard of the White ranch, they would be expecting the supply wagon to be arriving out there shortly, give or take half an hour.

That was not much time to do what else had to be done, but Walt did not worry very much. He was too pleased with what had already been accomplished. What had started out as an investigation of a couple of attempted murders—one of which had been aborted because the wrong victim was in a wagon —had ended up with the discovery of what was probably the biggest cattle rustling operation in northern New Mexico.

Rough knuckles rolled across his door and before he had a chance to respond Bertha Maloney entered, stopped to wrinkle her nose, then advanced upon the coal oil lamp to bring light into the room as she said, "Is Dr. Eaton treating you with horse liniment? It'll take a month to get that smell out of here." Before Walt could open his mouth she stopped at his bedside and asked if he could eat a decent meal—fried spuds, coffee, pot roast cooked with new onions. She stopped speaking only when her gaze fell upon the little belly-gun. She regarded it for a moment, but did not comment as she leaned and said, "I have a helper. She's a better cook than I am, Constable . . . She made an apple pie." The steely eyes were soft as Bertha Maloney smiled. "I'll have her fetch in your supper."

She walked out and closed the door before Walt had said whether he was up to that kind of a meal or not.

CHAPTER 16

The Passage of Time

WHEN Elizabeth Bartlett brought his supper her cheeks were red from kitchen heat. He waited for her to speak first, which she did not do until she had removed the belly-gun from his small bedside table and put the tray down. Then she turned and said, "I must go back to the neck tomorrow."

He nodded understanding.

"I . . . have two dollars. Can I hire a couple of men to dig the grave for that amount?"

Walt nodded again then said, "I'll have them rounded up for you in the morning."

She held her fingers locked together in front and regarded him solemnly. "I guess I shouldn't even have told you what happened at the spring."

He eyed the food; there was enough of it for a small army. "I don't know what to say, except that since you did tell me, we both know."

She pulled up the chair and sat down to help him eat. He was perfectly capable without her assistance but let her help him anyway.

He was starved but had been unaware of it until she had entered the room and the aroma reached him. As she watched him eat she said, "I'll shave you tomorrow if you wish, Constable."

He cast a sideways glance at her. "Did you ever shave anyone before?"

She nodded without speaking and he could have kicked himself for asking that question. He made an attempt to cover up the gaffe by agreeing that she could shave him and that he'd be grateful because his face itched from the unaccustomed growth. Then he said, "Elizabeth, what next?"

She looked him squarely in the eye when she replied. "That will be up to the local constable."

He reached for the coffee cup. "I meant—what would you like to do now? Would you like to go back to the homestead?"

She shook her head. "No. Never . . . I never want to see it again. I have an aunt back in Ohio somewhere but I haven't seen her since I was a small child. Before my mother died." Her gray-green eyes were fixed on his face. "Why did you ask? Constable Cutler, I am a murderer."

He stopped chewing and looked at her with annoyance. She turned away and became busy with a wedge of hot apple pie on a chipped plate. She removed his empty dishes and put the plate on his lap. "Too much cinnamon," she said. "I . . . it's not easy to bake a pie two days after your husband died."

He found nothing wrong with the pie at all. In fact he thought it was the best apple pie he could remember ever having eaten, but that may not have been much of a commendation because apple pies in his life had been very few and very far between. "Very good," he told her around a mouthful. "Just the right amount of cinnamon."

"Constable . . ."

"I don't want to talk about it, Elizabeth."

"I wasn't going to say anything about *that*, I was going to ask you if you knew Mr. McGregor from the bank told one of Missus Maloney's roomers that one of Mr. White's neighbors told him there was something peculiar going on out at the White ranch?"

Walt paused with the fork poised. "In Peralta, Elizabeth, you can hear anything if you just wait long enough." To himself he swore in silence even though whatever McGregor knew, or thought he knew, had come to the surface too late to make more trouble. At least he thought it had come too late. Unless he was mistaken Mack Kelso would be trying to backtrack his supply wagon about now, and even if he rode all the way down to Peralta in his search, by the time he reached town it would be late; Jim McGregor and a number of other residents of Peralta would not still be up and around.

He finished the pie, handed back the plate, and when their eyes met, something large enough to be painful turned over in his chest. She was a beautiful woman, even with dark shadows under her eyes. He said, "Could you find my shirt? I got some makings in a pocket and sure could use a smoke."

"Smoking isn't good for you, Mr. Cutler."

He had heard that before and gave her the answer he had given to others. "I'm sure it isn't. My grandpaw was sure it wasn't too."

She widened her eyes. "Your grandfather?"

"Yes'm. He told me tobacco wasn't good for folks right up to the day he died at one hundred and two."

She arose and became busy piling the empty plates. As she straightened up with her arms full she smiled to him. "I'll find your shirt and be back."

He watched her leave the room and sank back against the pillow. He was as full as a toad; he was almost uncomfortably full. Even when he hadn't been injured he had not eaten like that. But then, he hadn't eaten that kind of a woman-cooked meal either, which probably made a difference.

When the door opened he expected Elizabeth Bartlett. Instead it was Dr. Eaton with his black satchel which he put on the bedside table, then wrinkled his nose. "What have you been eating? It smells like a steak fried in horse liniment."

Walt watched Eaton peeling up his sleeves. "That's what it was. I thought you'd be back down to Mineral Wells by now."

"In another hour, Constable." Eaton straightened up, looking fierce. "You have the most unconscionable son of a gun managing the Peralta stage yard I've ever met. Yesterday he told me there'd be an afternoon stage. This afternoon he told me there would be no afternoon stage, just the night stage going south."

"What about your buggy?"

"The blacksmith couldn't get to it until late this afternoon and the wheel will not be ready until morning. Now put your hands behind your head . . . Have you any idea how much money I'm losing being stuck up here in Peralta? . . . How did this bandage get pulled loose; have you been trying to get out of bed?"

"Bandages work loose, don't they, Doctor?"

Eaton reared back scowling. "Do you have any idea how many years I've been at my trade, Constable? I know a wrenched bandage when I see one—and you're not going to admit that you tried to leave the bed. I know that too, from experience with men like you . . . Now hold still."

The aroma of cooked food and horse liniment disappeared as Dr. Eaton made liberal use of the disinfectant that smelled like carbolic acid. As he was working he said, "Mr. Tower was in a fight at the general store today. I just came from wrapping his knee. He's too old to be fighting."

Walt did not agree with that, he simply said, "How bad is his knee?"

"No worse than a horse-kick. Swollen and tender but he'll be fine in a week or so . . . The emporium's proprietor sat next to me at the café counter this evening and gave me a punch by punch account of that battle. He was still furious with Mr. Tower for starting a fight in his store . . . Well, Constable, you are a remarkably healthy individual. The wounds are closing very well. Better than I would have thought they might."

Walt eyed the busy older man. "That means I can ride in a—"

"It means no such thing," exclaimed the doctor. "You are healing very well and very fast. That's what it means. It also means that if you leave this bed you will probably have to be carried back here to it and be flat on your back for another five or six weeks."

Walt watched Dr. Eaton roll down his sleeves, snap his satchel closed and, straighten around to face the bed as he said, "You don't need me any further. There's a midwife in town, so I've been told, who can look after the dressings . . . Even the hearty soul who runs this rooming house can do that. You owe me six dollars."

Walt's eyes sprang wide open. "Six dollars! All you did was change a few bandages and pour that smelly stuff around."

Dr. Eaton was imperturbable. "Six dollars. One dollar of that is for the cloth and medicine, the rest of it's for professional services." Eaton's pursed lips remained in that expression for a moment, then they loosened. "Well, three of those dollars are for your care. The other three are for coming up here to look after that settler who died . . . The woman won't have money to spare for doctoring, don't you agree?"

Walt agreed. "I'll send six dollars down to you at Mineral Wells. I can't pay you now because I don't know where my pants are. My purse is in 'em."

Dr. Eaton made one of his brusque little birdlike nods and departed, the only evidence that he had been in the room the smell of carbolic acid and the itching where he had replaced Walt's old bandage with a fresh one.

When Elizabeth returned she did not mention that she had waited until the doctor had departed. She handed him a depleted sack of tobacco and a packet of brown papers, then she stood primly watching him roll and light his smoke. He grinned at her. She was not the same person he had ridden back to Peralta with in Kelly O'Bryon's spring wagon. She seemed calm, almost fatalistic. Her coloring was better and her stance was more erect. Whatever she had thought since yesterday morning, and he made no attempt to guess about that, she had a look about her of someone who had capably weathered a storm and was now ready for the next storm.

He gestured toward the chair and she sat down. The silence was a little awkward; he knew what was uppermost in her mind and he'd be damned before he'd bring it up. Instead, he said, "Bertha said you're a better cook than she is."

Elizabeth's gaze softly brightened at the compliment. "I'm not, of course. She's very kind . . . and motherly."

"And tough," added Walt, thinking of things he'd heard the rooming house owner say to some of her more forward customers.

"Isn't that what's required in New Mexico, Marshal, toughness?"

He exhaled at the ceiling. "I suppose so, but there are all kinds of toughness." When he lowered his eyes to her face she was regarding him a trifle sardonically. "Well," he added, "aren't there?"

She did not pursue this, she gazed toward the lamp and said, "It's a land of suffering, Constable."

He shied clear of becoming entangled in another discussion he thought would lead nowhere. "Elizabeth, I want you to stay. I like talking to you."

She returned her gaze to his face, and waited for what she knew was an inevitable return to the uppermost problem for both of them.

"Ron Sexton was an outlaw from Montana," he said. "Maybe he said something bad to you."

"No. I told you what he said; it was about our old horse. It was nothing personal."

Walt blew more smoke at the ceiling. "I wish you'd help me, Elizabeth."

"Mr. Cutler, I can't. I told you the truth as well as I remember it. It's not all clear in my mind. I was terribly upset and sick at heart when I walked all the way up to the spring. I don't really even remember walking all that distance. I don't believe you'd understand. Another woman would, not a man. Everything we'd dreamed and planned—everything we laughed about that was wonderful—all of it was going out of my life a day at a time and there was no way I could even hold it back for just one day. Everything . . ."

He heard the catch in her voice and did not look down from the ceiling. After a while he said, "I'll tell you something. This cigarette doesn't taste good."

She held forth a little dish for him to punch it out in, then set the dish aside and breathed deeply for a moment or two, for control.

He still did not face her. "I got to think of something, Elizabeth."

She studied his rugged profile. "If anyone can, Constable Cutler, I suspect you can do it." She arose. "But I doubt if it's been done before, has it? Find an excuse for murder?"

After she left him he tossed the tobacco and papers atop the bedside table and lay back to sleep. He was tired; not especially sleepy, but tired.

He was thinking of Elizabeth Bartlett when Fred Tower limped in from the hallway looking fresh, shaved, and cleanly dressed. He eyed the lawman as he headed for the chair. "You look a little worse every time I see you," Fred said bluntly. "I brought a pony of whiskey." Fred put the little bottle on the bedside table and eyed the lamp askance. "Don't anyone around here ever trim wicks and clean mantels?"

Walt allowed a moment to pass, then asked Fred to find some gravediggers to go out to the neck in the morning with Elizabeth Bartlett to bury her husband.

Fred fidgeted on the chair. "Walt, one of Gus's boys was over in that area this afternoon."

Cutler heard the drag in Tower's voice and turned his head.

His stare did not make things any easier for Fred Tower but he plunged ahead with what he had to say. "There's no need for her to go out there . . . Someone fired the log house. Gus's boy said it was burnt to the ground." Fred looked at Cutler. "I expect that'd mean her husband got cremated."

Walt let got a rattling sigh. "One more thing for her to have to know about," he said softly. "What does someone like Elizabeth Bartlett do to get this kind of treatment?"

Fred had no idea nor did he offer one. He instead changed the subject. "That's not what I come up here to talk to you about. That feller who works for the stage company and drives the southbound down from San Xavier—you know the one; he's got a set of up-curling whiskers."

Walt knew who Fred was talking about. "Yeah. What about him?"

"He was down at the corralyard gate as I was walking up here. He told me he saw a party of horsemen to the east of the road just a little shy of dusk. He said they was reading sign, wagon tracks he thought it was, and they were heading toward town.''

Walt put a smoky stare upon the older man and Tower looked directly back. Neither one of them had any doubts about who those riders were.

"How's the prisoner?" Cutler asked, and Fred shrugged wide shoulders. "Actin' like a trapped animal.''

Walt was thoughtful for a moment, then told Fred Tower what he thought should be done in Peralta before Kelso and his riders rode in.

CHAPTER 17

A Time for Worry

BERTHA MALONEY came in looking tired and plumped down upon the chair. She announced that there was absolutely nothing good about being a widow unless it was that a woman could sleep the night through without interruption, and she thought that was both a mixed blessing and an awful price to pay for being widowed.

Because in their years of friendship they had never been as personally close as they had been since Walt had been brought in wounded, and because he had never heard her say anything like this before and it embarrassed him, he groped around for the tobacco sack and papers.

Then she brought his head around by saying, "Some traders with a pack train came in a while ago for rooms. They told me they had seen smoke from about ten miles out and by the time they got closer, there was nothing left of a log house and a woodshed of someone's homestead."

Walt could see in her face that she knew whose log house that had been. He told her he knew; that Fred Tower had told him about a half hour earlier. Then he said, "Missus Maloney, what else can happen to her?"

The graying woman considered the lighted lamp as she said, "I don't know. I *do* know something about heart-ache and tragedy." The steely eyes swung back to Walt's face. "She's been talking about going out there tomorrow to bury her husband . . . Which one of us tells her, Mr. Cutler?"

He ignored the reflection of lamplight off the little nickel-plated belly-gun and trickled smoke. Bertha Maloney watched his face for a long time before she sighed and said, "You're right. It would be better if a woman told her."

He squinted at her. He hadn't said a word.

Bertha Maloney ignored the look. She was an individual who had learned harsh lessons in an environment which had never been mild; she did not linger over unpleasantness once it had been resolved and her mind had been made up. She said, "I have seven roomers. Three are overnighters but in some ways they're more work than the steady residents, and I'm getting tired. Maybe I'm getting too old, but from daylight to dark on a person's feet every hour is hard."

Walt stubbed out the quirley. Garrulousness was something he encountered quite often in his trade. He had learned to suffer through it in silence, which is what he did now until she said, "Elizabeth and I both came from the same territory back east. Quite a coincidence, isn't it? We talked about folks back there; she knew more of them than I did . . . Mr. Cutler, I'd like to sell the rooming house and go back there. Maybe just for a year or two until I'm rested up . . . I'd like her to make the trip with me. Get her away from this country, get her to breathe fresh air and see different land and trees and all."

Walt had just one question. "Has she agreed to go?"

"Oh Lord no. I haven't mentioned it. Just that maybe I'd sell out and go back myself. I never said a thing to her about goin' with me." Bertha Maloney put her head slightly to one side. "You know her best—should I ask her?"

He was silent so long Bertha fidgeted, then arose from the chair. When their eyes met, his were deeply troubled. Bertha stared at him as though something momentous had just occurred to her. She leaned and impulsively patted his hand and said, "Well, I had no idea it was like that, Mr. Cutler. It just never crossed my mind. Does Elizabeth know?"

"Know what?"

"Never mind. I won't say a word." As she headed for the door Bertha Maloney said, "It's about time. You got to be about thirty."

She closed the door after herself very gently, leaving Walt regarding it with a furrowed brow.

He dismissed Bertha Maloney's odd behavior in favor of some bittersweet thoughts about Elizabeth. The first time he had seen her, at least the first time they had faced each other, he had been stopped in his tracks by her beauty, her willowy litheness and the expression of something close to fatalistic acceptance in her eyes which made them look serene.

When she had cared for him out at the homestead, doing double duty and not once acting other than willing and compassionate, he had wondered at her strength and capability.

After he knew about her dying husband he marvelled even more. She was, he had told himself out there, one of the most thoroughly capable, disciplined women he had ever known. She was *the* most capable and disciplined, and handsome woman as well.

And she had killed a man.

Kelly O'Bryon walked in from the dingy hallway looking solemn as an owl. "There's trouble on the way," he said without the customary little civil preliminaries to conversation which were considered absolutely necessary in range country. "Fred took his hired man down to the jailhouse to identify Sackett. I guess poor old Jake liked to wet his pants when Sackett walked up to the front of the cell, grabbed the steel straps, and glared at him. But he identified Sackett as the feller who bought those tooled spur leathers."

Kelly went to the chair, but instead of sitting on it he leaned on the back of it, looking at Walt from a distance of about eight feet. "I guess we didn't really need Jake to identify Sackett, though, did we? And that's not what I came in to tell you . . . For some reason old Gus Heinz with his sons and their hired hands rode into town a little while ago—guns under their stirrup-leathers and around their middles. They stabled their animals with me down at the barn and wouldn't say no more than 'Howdy.' They're over at the saloon now." Kelly paused to let all this soak in before adding a little more. "Heinz never did get along with Kelso. In fact he never got along with old

John Alden White real well, despite what he says, and he don't even speak to his heir, that blustery feller who inherited the outfit . . . Walt, Fred told me Kelso's comin' with his riders."

Walt had to make an almost physical effort to get his attention away from what he had been thinking about before O'Bryon's visit. He eased his head back on the pillow and said, "I never felt so useless in my life, Kelly."

O'Bryon remained silent. He did not feel exactly elated himself. He had a lively imagination and it had been creating a frightening scenario in his mind since about suppertime when he and Fred had talked at the café counter.

Still leaning on the chair he said, "Old Heinz isn't someone who'll sit around a lot. I've known him a long time and when he don't like someone he don't like him all over. But I never saw him ride into Peralta like this before, guns stickin' out everywhere and those two big sons of his with faces that look like they been blasted out of pure rock. God help us if Kelso's in the same mood. They'll wreck this town, Walt."

The constable had not anticipated the return to Peralta of Gus Heinz with his men, all of them loaded for bear, but he had thought there might be trouble with Kelso, which was why he had asked Fred Tower to take a few local businessmen, such as Jim McGregor, aside and explain what Walt knew and what he feared might happen. Fred was to ask them to support the law and to pass word around that the law needed other local support as well.

He lay there now visualizing some of the looks Fred had got, and maybe some of the comments too: If bad trouble was coming Peralta need a lawman who could stand up to it, not one lying on his back at the rooming house unable to even pull on his britches.

Kelly did not like Walt's reaction or his mood. He shifted his leaning position on the chair and morosely eyed the little under-and-over hide-out gun. If a man came right down to it that thing was pretty useless too. It wasn't even accurate over fifty feet.

Walt broke into O'Bryon's thoughts with a question. "What time is it?"

O'Bryon pulled out his watch, flipped the case open, studied the spidery little black hands, and snapped the case closed as he said, "A little shy of nine o'clock." He then pocketed his watch and waited.

Walt raised up a little and looked around. "Find Gus and tell him I want to see him."

O'Bryon nodded. In his mind, being given an order under these circumstances indicated that the constable's mind was working, and that was all O'Bryon needed. He left the room moving briskly.

Walt pushed up straighter in the bed, breathed deeply a couple of times, then moved his injured leg and hip. The pain arrived instantly. Not as bad as it had been but he knew it would be as bad if he did more than just move the leg.

He swore fiercely but remained sitting up. At least that did not cause pain.

When Gus Heinz arrived he filled the doorway. Behind him was one of his big-boned, taffy-haired sons, a man Walt knew passably well. His name was Carl. He had a reputation on the range as a rough, tough, good-natured, hard-working individual. Walt had heard a rumor that Carl was sparking some girl in town but had never seen Carl with her, if the rumor were true, and had no idea who she might be.

Gus had an old Colt tied down on the right side. Carl's tied-down weapon was on the left side; that was something else Walt did not know about the young Heinz: He was left-handed.

He pointed to the chair and forced a smile at them. "It's the only one so you'll have to flip a coin for it," he said. Neither man smiled and although they advanced into the room neither of them even glanced at the chair.

Gus's strong, heavy features were set like iron. "You wanted to talk?" he said.

Walt's smile vanished. He gave Gus stare for stare. "Yeah. What are you doin' in town armed for a fight?"

Heinz was a direct man. "Because we know Mack Kelso's

comin' the same way with his whole crew an' they're armed to the gullet." Gus paused without softening his expression. "It'll take Mack maybe ten minutes to find out that you got one of his riders locked up. It won't take even that long for him to figure out why. I figured you bein' flat down and all, and the folks here in Peralta bein' mostly a mealy bunch, you might need some help. Anything wrong with that?"

There wasn't anything wrong with it up to a point. Walt shook his head. "No. But, Gus, feeling the way you do about the White ranch, Mack in particular . . ."

"Walt," growled the barrel-shaped older man, pale eyes like granite, "I never in my life went out to force a fight with anyone. You're right; I got no use for Mack. Didn't have even before I knew he was a cow thief and got even less use for him now. But we're goin' to stay over there in the saloon and mind our own business and wait. I know Kelso, Walt. I know him better'n you do."

"Meaning?"

"If he thinks for one minute that 'breed cowboy of his you got in the jailhouse told you about the rustling, and all the rest of it, he's goin' to bust that cowboy out of there, take him up into the mountains, and hang him from an oak tree. That'll be his openers. I don't know what else he'll do; maybe shoot you in that bed and maybe even fire the town. When Mack knows some of us know what him and those two saddle-tramps he's been peein' through the same knothole with have been up to—shootin' people in the bargain—take my word for it, Walt, you never saw his temper; he's going to go wild."

Carl Heinz stepped to the open window and leaned to look out, to the left then the right, as though what his father had been saying made him uneasy enough to worry about someone hiding out there listening. When he straightened up back inside the room he wagged his head then turned and perched on the sill in the same spot Mack Kelso's rangerider had sat. He did not offer a suggestion, any encouragement, nothing at all; he simply sat there gazing at the helpless man in the bed.

Walt's furrowed brow smoothed out as he said, "Gus, do me a favor."

"Sure. Glad to."

"Find Fred or Kelly and tell them to take that man out of the jailhouse and bring him up here to this room by the back alley so no one will know they're moving him."

Gus gave that some ponderous thought, during the course of which his little pale eyes landed upon the belly-gun. He pointed. "Is that all you got?"

Walt shrugged. "Yeah. Kelso's rider had it under his shirt."

Heinz was turning when he gruffly said, "It ain't enough. Come along, Carl."

Walt had about fifteen minutes to himself. He wanted to believe Gus Heinz would not push for a showdown with his old enemy, the White ranch, and perhaps Walt did not know Mack Kelso as well as Gus did, but he'd sat in on too many poker hands with Gus not to know *him*. For Gus to stay out of whatever trouble arrived in town when Kelso and his men rode in, would require a degree of restraint Walt did not believe the tough old cowman possessed, especially since he had an equal armed force behind him.

As for Kelso, Walt's plan was simple. He wanted Frank Sackett with him in his room because he intended for someone to whisper to Kelso that this was where his errant rangerider was. He wanted to face Kelso himself, standing up or flat on his back. Walt Cutler was the Law; this whole mess was his responsibility.

As Gus had stated, that belly-gun was not the best of weapons although in this room it fit perfectly because that's what belly-guns were made for, shooting at a target which was no farther away than the hall doorway.

Walt reached for the little gun, broke it, looked at the pair of big bullets, snapped it closed, and casually folded the upper part of a blanket over it with his hand underneath. He would have felt better if he'd had six bullets instead of two, but he knew that anyone walking in on him with fire in their eyes and suspicion in their mind would notice the bulge of a larger weapon.

Common sense told him it was a poor weapon to bet a life on. But if common sense was so smart it should have warned him not to walk along the back of that log house where a man named Sawyer Kent had nearly killed him.

CHAPTER 18

"You're Crazy!"

WHEN Frank Sackett entered the room accompanied by both Kelly O'Bryon and Fred Tower, whose limp was a little less noticeable than it had been in the early afternoon, Walt told Sackett to stand against the wall away from the door. Then he eyed Fred and Kelly. "I guess you know about Gus being in town. Fred, did you pass the word around that we might need some backing?"

Tower eyed the chair as he answered. "Yeah. Started at the saloon and worked my way south. I'd say mostly they'll do what they can, but there's some, like McGregor, who haven't handled a gun in years." Fred's eyes showed a faintly ironic twinkle. "This may well turn out to be a case where a man might be in more danger from his friends than his enemies."

Walt smiled a little then turned his attention upon the rangerider. "You're going to stay in here with me, because someone around town will tell Kelso you've been in custody since early afternoon." Walt paused to watch Sackett's expression. He did not have to wait long; Sackett's features showed an increasing sense of anxiety. Walt pointed toward the baseboard and said, "Sit down and stay down."

Sacket sat on the floor, knees drawn up, looking from Walt to the other men. He suddenly said, "I could be a hunnert miles from here come daylight."

Fred eyed him sourly. "Which way—up or down?" He then faced the bed again. "I got a bad feeling about this, Walt, and the Heinz outfit being in town don't make it any better."

If there was one thing Walt Cutler did not especially need at this juncture it was gloom. He said, "Heinz will be over at the saloon. He told me he figured to stay over there and keep out of it."

Fred snorted but said nothing. O'Bryon was not that taciturn: "And suppose Kelso walks into the saloon?"

Walt picked that up instantly. "That's what I want to talk to you boys about. Someone can be leanin' on the rack out front and when Kelso gets down to tie up, someone can whisper to him that his rangeman is up here in my room at the rooming house, keeping me company because I can't get up."

Fred's eyes widened but none of his other features moved. Kelly O'Bryon peered from narrowed eyes in the direction of the bed. "Here?" he said incredulously. "Are you crazy?"

Fred Tower's features suddenly turned crafty. "He's not crazy, Kelly. Me and you'll be just outside that window. We can get another four or five men to hide out there with us. Right, Walt?"

Walt's delayed response was caused by doubts he had about situations of this kind. Planning in advance was an excellent course of action for a church social or maybe even a horseshoe-pitching contest because folks were in an agreeable mood and could be steered around. This was not going to be a horseshoe-pitching contest.

"No one will be outside the window, Fred. Kelso'll see that open window the minute he enters this room. I want him to come in here alone. Can you and Kelly round up those men you spoke of and have them come in behind Kelso's riders and throw down on them?"

Fred looked steadily at Cutler. "That won't work. Walt, if there's a crowd around when they tie up . . . Kelso's not an idiot."

O'Bryon's eyes lit up. "Gus—in the saloon. He could simply walk out with his riders holding guns in their hands, and Fred and I can then walk Kelso up here."

Tower did not like that either. He glowered at the liveryman. "Heinz comes out of the Horseshoe with a gun in his hand and there'll be a massacre. What's the matter with you, Kelly? Those two outfits been champin' at the bit to have a run at one another for years."

O'Bryon reddened. "Then you come up with something," he snapped.

Tower faced the bed again. In his near-drawling manner of speaking he said, "We can see to it Mack is told where Sackett is, an' I expect Kelso'll come up here. But he won't do it alone. Maybe the window is the best idea after all, Walt . . . Only you're goin' to be a sittin' duck if trouble starts, lyin' in that bed and all."

Sackett, whose dark eyes had been jumping from speaker to speaker, had good reason to feel desperate. It required no great intellect to understand that in Sackett's predicament, with both factions after his hide, no matter which faction survived a confrontation, he was going to lose. He straightened up along the wall and spoke directly to Constable Cutler.

"Mack don't know I'm a prisoner. If you tell him it'll be the dumbest thing you can do. Just say the team ran away with the supply wagon, the rig overturned, and some fellers fetched me back to town with a busted leg and I'm up here being looked after by the doctor."

Three sets of eyes went to Sackett's face and remained there until O'Bryon made a wide grin and said, "Walt . . . ? Kelso knows something happened to the wagon."

Fred Tower shifted all the weight off his injured leg and looked dourly thoughtful before wagging his head and offering a less enthusiastic point of view. "Maybe. Just maybe it was too dark for them to see there was only one set of tire marks—the one Sackett made comin' to town . . . Maybe they might believe such a story. If they thought the wagon overturned on the outskirts somewhere." Fred flapped his arms. The problem of planning a deception and then having it work had just occurred to him too. He ended up by saying, "I don't know . . . I do know if Gus Heinz comes out of the Horseshoe it's goin' to be like the Fourth of July." He gazed at Walt. "All right, we'll see to it Kelso finds out his rider is here in the rooming house . . . Walt, never in gawd's green world is he goin' to walk into this room alone so's you can arrest him."

"Even if he don't know I'm in here with Sackett, Fred, and even if he don't think there's anything wrong?"

Tower remained adamant. "Even then. We can stand around talkin' until the cows come home and when it comes right down to it—let Kelly and me round up a few boys and hide out in the dark beyond the window." Tower's dark eyes looked almost mournful. "You don't have to do this, Walt. You don't have to prove anything to this town."

Walt's face reddened a little but in the poor lamplight his friends probably did not see this. It was his responsibility; standing up or flat down he was the Law in Peralta and it was his job to perform as the Peralta Lawman. "Six months from now no one is goin' to say I was in bed when hell busted loose and left it up to the town to put out the fire."

Fred rolled his eyes in an expression of exaggerated dismay. "I thought you were more level-headed than to say something like that," Tower exclaimed.

For a moment or two there was silence. Both Fred and Kelly could tell from Cutler's expression this was his stand and he was not going to budge from it.

Fred was turning toward the door when he said, "And I thought bulls was pigheaded." He paused to look aside at Frank Sackett; with a leveled finger and a baleful glare he offered some advice to the rangeman. "You're goin' to be one unhealthy son of a gun if you so much as look crossways when Kelso comes in here . . . I owe you one anyway."

When they were alone Sackett asked if he could sit on the chair and Walt shrugged; then under the rangeman's gaze he made a careless-looking lump of the covers and put his hand under them holding the little belly-gun. He cocked it beneath the blankets and Sackett's eyes jumped to his face. Walt said, "You better hope this thing shoots."

Sackett did not remark about his belly-gun, he had something else in mind. "There'll be four of 'em if the whole crew comes along." His black eyes moved around the poorly lighted drab room. "Constable, the man I kicked in the knee was right—look at this place—a fly couldn't hide in here."

Walt did not look around the room; he already knew every crack in the floor and every knot in the wall panelling. "No one is going to hide," he told Sackett.

For a long while the prisoner sat slumped. Just once did he straighten on the chair. That was when he thought he heard a faint rustling sound outside the back-wall window. He twisted around as tense as a coiled spring and when he eventually faced forward again he was desperate. His chair was in line with the window. It was also in line with the door. If a fight started he was going to get shot from in front and maybe also from the back. He said, "Constable, you can tie me or chain me, but not in this room." When Walt did not respond the cowboy leaned and spoke in an impassioned voice. "I'll tell you somethin' you'd give a lot to know if you'll have 'em put me in another room."

Looking doubtful, Walt eyed Sackett's sweat-shiny dark face. "You've already told me all I got to know to lock Kelso up and throw away the key."

"But there's more," Sackett exclaimed, leaning forward. "If you want to face 'em with just my belly-gun that's up to you, but me—I don't even have a stick. The minute you say something to Mack about rustling cattle he's going to know where it come from—I can't even protect myself."

Walt's gaze hardened upon the rangerider. "I'll bet someone a new hat I got your face on a wanted dodger down at the jailhouse. Fred and Kelly were supposed to bring the box of posters up here and forgot to, but I'd bet new money your face is in that box. You're not going out of here and if you try it I'll use up one of the bullets in your gun stopping you."

Sackett remained poised upon the edge of the chair. If he had some frantic notion about jumping the man in the bed, he did not have it after Walt moved his fists from beneath the blankets so that the faint but recognizable big bore of the .44 belly-gun was aimed from a distance of no more than eight or nine feet.

He eased back in the chair and said, "I'll tell you anyway:

We been pickin' up some of Heinz's cattle about five or six miles north on his range and addin' them to our own drives."

Walt stared. Obviously Gus did not realize he had been getting raided too, and if he found out about it tonight when the White-ranch riding crew, rustlers to a man, rode into town, nothing under the sun—or the moon—would stop the Heinzes from precipitating a war in Peralta's main roadway.

Walt started violently when his door opened. It was Elizabeth. She stopped in the doorway holding a coffee pitcher and cup and stared at Frank Sackett. Her color drained away. In a whisper she said, "Walt, that's the man who looked back as they were riding toward the woodshed after firing through the door."

Sackett did not seem to be breathing. He did not take his eyes off Elizabeth Bartlett even after she had gone around upon the far side of the bed to put the pot and cup on the little bedside table.

She did not look at Sackett again; she stood slightly sideways facing the man in the bed. The shock at seeing one of the horsemen who had attacked the log house had chased something else out of her eyes, but as she recovered from shock and stood looking down, Walt saw the haunted look return. She knew someone had fired the log house with her dead husband's body inside it.

In a distant voice she asked if he would like something to eat before she and Bertha retired for the night. He held her gaze and softly smiled upwards while shaking his head. "No thanks an' I appreciate you thinkin' about it."

She did not return his smile and as she turned toward the door she did it so that she would be facing away from Sackett. After the door closed the rangeman leaned forward on the chair looking stonily at the floor. Walt filled the single cup with black coffee and held it out. "Drink it," he said.

When Sackett raised his face and reached for the cup and met the lawman's eyes, he found not one shred of warmth in them.

Sackett drained the cup and was holding it away when

he cocked his head. He almost whispered the word, "Horses."

Walt also heard them but not until they had come farther down from the north end of town. It sounded like at least four of them and they were being ridden at a walk.

Sackett put the cup aside, shot a desperate look over his shoulder in the direction of the window—and saw something Walt could not see. Whatever it was made Sackett face forward on the chair and abandon any desperate notion he might have been entertaining of taking a chance and diving head-first out the window.

He met the constable's eyes with a grimace and a wag of the head. "I'll tell you something, Mr. Cutler—it ain't just me who's goin' to hell on foot if there ain't a miracle tonight . . . I don't think you're brave, I think you're crazy. Sawyer Kent's the fastest man with a six-gun I ever knew. If Mack comes through that door Sawyer will be right behind him."

Walt got sarcastic. "Anything else I ought to know? Maybe Kent's blind on one side or something?"

Sackett looked steadily at Cutler. In an almost inaudible voice he said, "You really are crazy. Constable. If there's a fight, for Chrissake, you got two bullets. Between Mack and Sawyer they got at least ten. And if the other fellers come up here with them—"

Walt continued to eye the rangy dark man from an expressionless face. "Get down and pray if you want to," he told Sackett, "otherwise shut up. I want to hear anyone walkin' down the hall from out front."

Sackett rolled a cigarette with both elbows resting on his upper legs. He lighted it the same way. He was in the act of exhaling gray smoke when someone slammed a door down in the direction of the front porch, and there was a steady-paced roll of heavy boots coming in the direction of Walt Cutler's door.

Sackett stopped smoking. He seemed to have almost stopped breathing. His eyes were riveted to the door, his body was hunched with tension.

Walt gently swivelled the belly-gun beneath the blankets to face the door and counted the cadenced approach of those booted feet.

CHAPTER 19

A
Dead Man!

WHEN the footfalls stopped just short of the door a woman's voice was clearly audible to the men behind the door. Walt recognized the voice and its unfriendly tone as Bertha Maloney said, "The rooming house is closed for the night. If you need a place to bed down try the liverybarn; they got a hay loft."

There were several seconds of silence before the man spoke. "Which room belongs to the constable?"

Walt could visualize Bertha blocking the hall with her burly stance when she replied. "He's asleep. It's late and—"

"Lady, I know what time it is. Which room?"

The porch door opened and closed again. This time it sounded like more than one man entering the rooming house from the roadway. Walt saw Sackett stiffen on the edge of the chair and shot him a warning look.

The other men in the hallway came up and halted. Bertha seemed at a loss; at least she said nothing until the man who had spoken addressed the men around him. "Look in the rooms." Bertha's reaction to this was given in a raised tone of voice. "Don't you open a single door! Get out of here, all of you!"

The man she had been speaking to, who had a quiet, slightly harsh voice, said, "Which room—or we'll rout out every tenant you got!"

Walt and Sackett heard the sounds of scuffling and one profane exclamation before the scuffle ended. Silence returned and drew out until a softer, younger female voice said, "I'll use it." The silence returned. Walt and Sackett were motionless and tense.

The harsh-voiced man said, "Lady, put that shotgun down."

The answer he got told Cutler and Sackett all they had to know. "I've seen you. That man behind you, I've seen him too." The next sound was of both hammers on a double-barreled shotgun being cocked. "That's Mr. Cutler's door on your left."

The silence settled again. Walt had no difficulty understanding the dilemma of those men in the hallway. With a cocked scattergun aimed at them from probably no more than fifteen feet they were probably scarcely even breathing. At that range a double-barreled shotgun could cut an oak barrel in half; it would do even worse damage to human beings.

Elizabeth spoke again. "Open the door. You want to see the constable, open the door."

"Lady," the quiet-spoken man said, "all I want is to talk to the constable. Not with a shotgun aimed at me."

"I told you to open the door. *Do it!*"

Walt saw the latch rise, watched the door swing slowly inwards, and met the hooded, guarded eyes of Mack Kelso. The rangeboss's face was malevolently taut as he glanced at Frank Sackett, then back at Constable Cutler.

Walt tightened his grip on the hide-out gun as he said, "Come in."

The man crowding in behind Kelso was wiry, older than the rangeboss, and had a permanently bronzed set of thin features. His mouth was a wide gash. The other men would have pushed into the room also but Elizabeth stopped them. "Stay back. Line up along the wall."

Walt caught a partial glimpse of her. She was wearing a long bathrobe, holding the cocked shotgun in both hands, her profile half in hallway shadows. Bertha was nowhere in sight. He could not see the men Elizabeth had lined up against the wall. The man behind Mack Kelso turned his head to glance over his shoulder. If this man was Sawyer Kent, and if Frank Sackett was to be believed, he was deadly with the gun on his right hip. Elizabeth was not looking in the direction of the room, she was watching her captives. Walt did not allow the sinewy man the time to consider drawing on Elizabeth. He removed the cocked belly-gun from beneath the blankets as he said, "You! Face forward. Both of you come away from the door."

Kelso obeyed, which left the sinewy older man little choice. He also obeyed, but his tawny brown eyes were like wet agate as he looked at Walt and the little gun.

Kelso'd had time to think. He ignored everything behind him and gestured toward Sackett. "They told us he was hurt . . . I never believed that, Cutler."

The sinewy man, too, seemed to have lost interest in what was happening outside in the dingy hallway. He never once took his eyes off the man in the bed holding the belly-gun.

Kelso spoke again in the same quiet, slightly harsh tone of voice. "You set this up, didn't you? Why?"

Walt considered the rangeboss. He had known Mack Kelso several years. They had never been particularly friendly. For one thing Kelso rarely came to Peralta except occasionally on a Saturday night to let off a little steam with his riders. For another, Walt had never been able to sublimate or define his dislike of the man. It was just one of those feelings men occasionally had, there was no real reason for it.

Walt gestured with the cocked belly-gun. "Drop it and be careful."

Kelso's lips pulled back in a hard smile. He made no move to disarm himself. "Hidin' behind skirts, Constable?"

"I said shed that gun, Mack!"

Kelso continued to smile. "Naw, I don't think so. You're not goin' to shoot anyone, Cutler. A man who'd hide behind a skirt won't shoot someone face to face, will they?" Kelso turned his head toward Frank Sackett, still wearing his murderous smile. "What you doing in here, Frank?"

Sackett still had the dead and forgotten brown-paper cigarette between his lips. "They brought me in here, Mack. That old bastard who owns the saddle works jumped me in the general store, then they locked me up, and finally they brought me up here."

The rangeboss's dark eyes did not blink. He regarded Sackett with the intense stare of a rattlesnake. Walt saw something in

Kelso he had never seen before, or even suspected. Gus Heinz had warned him that Kelso had a terrible temper, and right at this moment Walt believed it. But Kelso was restraining himself. He had to.

"Frank, you and the constable here been having a long talk?" The rangeboss asked in that quiet, harsh voice.

Sackett's shirtfront was dark with sweat and it was not a warm night. His eyes were fixed on Kelso. "They been askin' a lot of questions," Sackett replied. "I didn't tell 'em a thing."

The wiry man finally stopped staring at Walt and faced Sackett, his lipless wide mouth drawn back in a snarl. "You lyin' bastard, Frank . . . you let us ride right into this."

Sackett removed the dead cigarette with a shaking hand and dropped it. He did not look at the wiry man. "What could I do, Sawyer? I been locked up. If I could have got loose I'd have—"

Out in the hall there was a violent explosion. It was deafening. It also broke the mood of leashed violence inside the room. The wiry man's movement was a blur of speed as he took one sidewards step and dropped his right shoulder. Walt squeezed the trigger of the belly-gun. This second explosion was almost as loud. The wiry man reacted to being hit as though he were a wound-tight steel spring; he half spun to his left with the gun in his hand already rising. His eyes bulged and did not appear able to maintain their focus. He struggled against falling, lost his battle, and went down, the six-gun in his right fist discharged from a spasmodic jerking of his muscles. The slug tore through the floor.

Sackett had jumped to his feet at the first explosion out in the hall. He took two steps and launched himself through the window. Mack Kelso had been drawing his gun, glaring wildly at the man in the bed, but Sackett's sudden movement distracted him. He shifted position slightly and pulled off a shot. Window glass flew in all directions but Sackett was no longer in sight.

Walt yelled: "*Mack!*"

Kelso twisted, gun gripped in his fist but uncocked. The belly-gun was aimed at his chest and it was cocked. Mack

Kelso had always been a man who thought fast. He became absolutely still.

Walt gave an order. *"Drop it!"*

Gently the rangeboss opened his hand to allow the six-gun to strike the floor with a solid sound.

Black-powder smoke was spreading in the room, drifting toward the broken window. The smell was like tanning acid.

Bertha Maloney appeared in the doorway holding an old long-barreled colt with the hammer fully back. Her hair was awry and her face was red. Walt looked from her face to the old gun. "Point it in some other direction," he said, and when Bertha had complied he said, "Elizabeth . . . ?"

Bertha jerked her head sideways. "She's all right . . . Are you?"

Walt nodded. "Yeah. I'm all right. Bertha, go hunt up Fred Tower, will you?"

She nodded, hesitated, gazing at Mack Kelso, at the dead man on the floor, then walked into the room, over to the bed, and put her long-barreled old six-gun on the covers. Without a word she then marched out of the room.

Walt and the rangeboss looked at one another. Kelso said, "Don't you have any men in this town; always got to hide behind skirts?"

Walt's relief that it was over made him watery in the knees, but since he was already on his back he was the only one who knew this.

A hatless head appeared through the broken window. O'Bryon said, "Fred's goin' around front, Bertha'll meet him at the door." Kelly looked at the dead gunfighter, then more briefly at the disarmed rangeboss before he said, "I didn't mean to hit the 'breed so hard on the head but when he come flyin' through the window it startled me." Kelly paused to look back and downwards at something on the ground. "They got thick skulls, don't they?"

The rangeboss finally moved a little. He went to the chair and, with one hand on the back of it, looked over his shoulder at the dead man. He remained like that for a long moment before facing Walt again.

Walt said, "Sit down. Sackett lied to you. He told us about the cattle stealing. He told us a lot more, Mack." Kelso looked contemptuous. "Frank never told the truth if a lie would do better."

"You got a surprise when you stopped O'Bryon's wagon, didn't you?"

"What are you talkin' about, Cutler?"

"About me being in the back instead of the settler. Mack, when it comes to lyin' I don't think Sackett'll be able to hold a candle to you. I'm going to lock you up and feed you beans and water for as long as it takes for you to tell me the truth about a lot of things."

The porch door was wrenched violently open and allowed to slam behind someone moving down the hall with a thrusting stride. The long stride abruptly halted and a voice Walt knew belonged to Fred Tower said, "Missus Bartlett, are you all right?"

Elizabeth replied shakily. "Yes. I wasn't holding it right . . . The recoil knocked me against the wall. My elbow hurts a little."

Fred made a little sympathetic sound before raising his voice. "Get flat down on the floor on your bellies." Evidently someone out there was slow to obey. Walt heard the meaty sound of a blow landing, followed by a body bouncing off wood to the floor.

Tower appeared in the doorway standing solidly on both legs, eyes bright and staring. He regarded Walt for a moment, then looked elsewhere. He considered the dead man the longest, barely more than acknowledged Kelso's presence, and came into the center of the room before he spoke. "You should have shot him when he refused to drop his pistol."

Walt nodded. For someone who had disliked the idea of hiding out back beyond the window, Fred must have been very close or he would not have heard the exchange between Kelso and Cutler over Kelso's sidearm. He eased the hammer down on the belly-gun and let it lie in his lap. "What happened out in the hall?"

Fred went to the chair and with one big hand yanked Kelso out of it, shoved him away, and sat down. Evidently during the excitement he had forgotten about his knee, and just as clearly the knee was now letting him know it was still injured. "I don't know what caused her to fire, but it sure put the fear of gawd into those men—and there's a hole in the wall you could throw a dog through."

"She didn't hit anyone?"

"No. She should have but the charge went wide."

"Why did she fire?"

Fred had no idea and did not think it was very important. He jerked a thumb in the dead man's direction. "What happened to him?"

"Went for his gun," stated Walt, and gazed at Mack Kelso. "I'd take it kindly if you'd lock Mack up and the rest of them."

Tower regarded the rangeboss stonily, said nothing, and scooped up the six-gun Kelso had dropped, shoved it into his waistband, and stepped to the window to lean down and call out. "Hey, Kelly! You fellers meet me around front." As he straightened up facing into the room Fred wagged his head. "I think Kelly got the fright of his life when that 'breed came flying right at him through the window . . . Kelso, pick up your dead friend there, and let's go."

The rangeboss was already moving when Walt stopped him with a question. "Which one of you burnt the settler's log house?"

Kelso looked malevolently at Walt without replying, then got Sawyer Kent over his shoulder and turned toward the door. As Fred Tower started after him past the bed he threw Walt a hard look and said, "Don't want to talk much, does he? I guarantee you by sunup the son of a gun'll be spouting off like a preacher."

CHAPTER 20

Toward Dawn

ELIZABETH leaned the doorway with her eyes upon Walt. He smiled at her. "What happened out there?"

"It just went off," she replied. "It was getting heavy so I started to shift my grip on it; it was pointing to the left away from those men, and it went off." She stepped back, lifted the shotgun from its leaning position against the wall, and brought it to him.

He held it warily. It still had one hammer cocked back. He eased the hammer down very gently and wagged his head. Elizabeth went to the chair and sank down. She was shaking.

Walt shucked out the spent casing and the loaded one, then tested the hammers. Evidently someone had filed the springs because both hammers responded to the slightest tug. He wagged his head again, put the gun aside, and looked at her.

"Are you all right, Elizabeth?"

She made a little face. "Yes, but when it fired the recoil slammed me against the wall. I bumped my elbow . . . It was so loud, Walt."

He had an almost irresistible urge to laugh. "Inside a house they sound like a cannon."

Bertha Maloney came into the room clutching her bathrobe. She saw the shotgun and let go a loud gust of spent breath. "I forgot it was in your room, Elizabeth. It belonged to my husband. I was always afraid of it because he told me he'd fixed the triggers to go off at a touch. Something about shooting quail—you have to shoot fast when they're on the rise." Bertha regarded the younger woman. "Does your arm hurt?"

Elizabeth smiled with her eyes. "Not very much. I never fired a shotgun before. I knew they had a recoil, but . . ."

Walt looked from one of them to the other. For some reason they put him in mind of a mother and a daughter. Maybe it was their concern for each other. He said, "Bertha, I heard scuffling before Elizabeth came out of her room with the shotgun."

For a fleeting moment Bertha's eyes flashed, then she moved to the side of the bed and perched there. "One of them grabbed me. I suppose to keep me from interfering if they started opening doors. I bit his arm as hard as I could and he released me." Bertha looked at the sticky dark stain on the floor, then looked at the broken window. "This room looks like someone's been butchering pigs in it . . . Constable, what happened?"

Walt told them, then he said, "You two could have got yourselves hurt."

Bertha was more interested in the rest of it. "Who were those men? I think I've seen the one who asked which room was yours. I think I've seen him around town. Constable, why were they looking for you?"

It was a long story; by Walt's reckoning it had to be about two o'clock in the morning. "Go to bed, ladies; maybe tomorrow we can talk about it . . . Thank you both."

Elizabeth arose first, holding her elbow with the opposite hand. "The two who came into your room were with that man you had locked up when the three of them attacked our house at the homestead, Constable."

Walt nodded. "I know . . . Good night—and thanks again."

When the door was closed and he was alone, Walt leaned the shotgun aside, put Bertha's hogleg Colt on the little bedside table, and picked up the belly-gun. A .44 bullet at that distance would have killed a man twice the size of Sawyer Kent; it could kill a horse at that distance, dead in his tracks. He put the little weapon beside the much larger handgun and settled back against the pillow.

There was chilly air coming in through the broken window, the house was silent except for an occasional creaking, groaning sound as old wood contracted after the heat of a very long day.

Gus Heinz had kept his word, he had remained over at the saloon. At least as far as Walt knew he had. He certainly had not rushed over to the rooming house when the firing began.

The reason Gus and a number of other men had not rushed to the rooming house was because after gun-thunder alerted them to trouble, it had ended very quickly and suddenly. They were out front when Fred and the townsmen he had rounded up herded Mack Kelso and his riders out onto the porch. The sight of Kelso carrying a dead man over his shoulder held the latecomers rooted and Fred did not allow even a pause as he herded the captives down to the jailhouse.

Gus Heinz walked in the direction of the liverybarn where he told his sons and hired riders to get saddled up. After all the riding he'd done today, which had ended up in nothing more than some noise and cussing, they all needed some sleep. He did not tell them that he was disappointed in how things had turned out. All afternoon he had been anticipating telling Mack Kelso exactly what he thought of him—and his ranch. As they cleared town in a slow lope for home old Gus shook his head. He did not know what had happened in the rooming house but he did know that Kelso and his crew were in jailhouse cells, and while he would have preferred to see them on their way to a much hotter place, he would have to accept the way things had turned out. At least the cow thieves were behind bars.

Gus was one of those individuals whose minds clung doggedly to dead issues in a brooding way for a long while after the dust had settled. But he had not become a successful cattleman by allowing something like that to prevent him from working his land and cattle. A man could work and brood at the same time.

As he saw the ranchyard through the chill clear air of false dawn his mind turned instinctively to the work that had to be done, now that this other mess had been concluded. As they were all unsaddling out front of the log barn he told his sons they would make up for lost time in the morning by heading northwest to the summer range to look over the first-calf heifers.

The stars were fading and to the east, where sawteeth rims pressed starkly against the horizon, a jagged paleness lay behind each upthrust. It was the pre-dawn light of a new day.

But not everyone slept. In fact probably very few people did. Fred and Kelly, with two jolt-glasses and a nearly empty bottle between them down at the jailhouse office, were wide awake. Kelly was still worried about the man he had struck over the head, who was now lying out full length on a cot in one of the cells with blood-matted hair and a bump the size of a goose egg.

Kelly thought Sackett should have regained consciousness long ago; he was sure he had busted Sackett's skull but Fred Tower, seated in Walt Cutler's chair behind the desk, sipped whiskey and propped his sore leg upon a little table as he said, "He asked for it . . . The fool." Fred considered the little glass he was holding. "That lady . . . Y'know, Kelly, I never saw one like her before. I can't right off hand think of very many men who'd have walked out to face those bastards, all of 'em armed, like she did."

O'Bryon nodded and sipped whiskey, and it was beginning to diminish his anxieties. His mind drifted from one aspect of what had happened to another and except for his part in things none of it particularly stood forth. It was good whiskey too. "Nothing came out the way we figured," he said. "Old Heinz —the other fellers around town . . ." Kelly drained his glass and leaned to place it beside the bottle on the desk. "That's malt whiskey, isn't it?"

Fred had to pick up the bottle and scowl over the label before nodding his head. He'd found the bottle on a shelf behind some law books in the office. "Yeah, it's malt whiskey . . . Kelly, that dead man in the back room—we was supposed to find Walt's box of dodgers and take 'em up to him. Suppose we was to look through those posters. I'm not sleepy, are you?"

Kelly was gazing at the pot-bellied stove near the far wall when he replied. He acted as though he had not heard anything Tower had said. "Something I'd like to know, Fred: Who fired the settler's log house?"

Fred was studying the nearly empty bottle and replied slowly. "That is good whiskey for a fact."

Kelly turned lowered brows. "Are you drunk, Fred?"

Tower hauled straight up in the chair. "You never saw me drunk, and you never will. I can handle whiskey like it's water rolling off a duck's back."

"Let's go roust those bastards up and find out who fired the settler's house."

Tower abandoned the notion he'd had about refilling his glass. He shifted slightly on the chair, shot his friend a look. "Maybe they wouldn't know," he said, and Kelly stared at him.

"They'd know. Who else would do that? You're damned right they know." Kelly arose, and stood motionless for a moment before saying, "Come on. And fetch that ring of keys."

"Well . . . In the morning, Kelly. It ain't something we got to know right now in the middle of the night."

O'Bryon stood with narrowed eyes studying Tower. He arrived at a conclusion and said, "Fred, you're drunk."

Tower, having scoffed at any such idea moments before, had his truthfulness to defend so he scowled at the liveryman. "How could anyone get drunk on what was in that bottle?" He leaned to rise, hung a moment, then abandoned the notion and sank back. He *was* drunk and if he arose from the chair his legs would wobble; if he didn't fall he would not be able to walk straight and Kelly would know he was drunk. He smiled at O'Bryon. "You go talk to them. My knee is giving me hell."

Kelly's gaze was sardonic. It wasn't the knee but he did not feel like making an issue of this so he said, "Hand me that ring of keys."

Fred obeyed. "Leave your six-gun here," he told the liveryman. That annoyed O'Bryon. "I'm not going to go in among them."

"Then what do you need the keys for?" Fred demanded.

Kelly looked at the ring of keys in his hand and flung it down atop the desk, hitched at his shellbelt, and went across the room to the bolt-studded, massive old oaken cell-room door. As he swung it open Fred Tower gently shook his head; he'd been told a number of times Indians and Irishmen could not handle whiskey. Well, Kelly didn't even weave as he crossed to the door.

Fred watched his friend heave the heavy door wide. Kelly took one step forward and collapsed as limp as a rag. Fred leaned over the desk looking owlishly downward. He continued to do this for several moments, then eased back in the desk chair wagging his head sympathetically. It was a fact after all: Irishmen could not handle whiskey.

He closed his eyes.

The sun struck first through two little barred windows in the jailhouse. The light awakened Fred Tower. He fished for something to dab at his eyes with. His mouth tasted like the floor of a Mexican barracks and his body ached from sleeping in a chair.

Kelly was not in the office. Fred eased his sore leg to the floor, tested it, then stood up. He had no headache but there were caterpillars in his belly. He limped to the cell-room door and squinted through the dingy gloom. There was no sign of Kelly and the prisoners stared back at him. He closed the door, dropped the *tranca* back into place, and crossed to the roadway door. He was opening it when Kelly O'Bryon stepped up to do the same from the outside. He held out a big crockery mug of steaming black coffee. Without a word passing between them they returned to the seats they had used last night, each with a cup of hot black java. Kelly had shaved and his eyes were clear. Fred scowled at him. "You passed out over yonder last night."

Kelly smiled. "How would you know? When I went home you were snoring."

They sipped coffee. When Fred's eyes fell upon their sticky jolt-glasses and the nearly empty bottle he swept them away into a desk drawer and finished the coffee. He lacked a lot of wanting to dance a fandango but the coffee did away with the caterpillars. "Go see if that feller you hit is dead yet," he told the liveryman but this time said nothing about leaving the gun on the desk as Kelly went briskly over into the cell room.

Fred's knee was more painful this morning than it had been

at any time yesterday; he blamed this condition on having propped his leg on that little table last night.

Voices came up to him from the cell room but he preferred not to listen to them. Right at this moment if the Angel Gabriel had walked in from out in the road, wings and all, Fred would not have spoken to him.

When O'Bryon returned and after he had closed and barred the cell-room door after himself, he said, "Sawyer Kent. But he didn't know there was anyone inside."

Fred considered this notion with a scowl. "Sawyer Kent's dead. Naturally they'd say it was him."

"I believe them, Fred. Kent and Sexton were partners. A man'd do something like to avenge his partner." Kelly eyed the larger and darker man with a suppressed twinkle. "Let's go over to the café. You need something to eat. If a man don't mind the grease, the cafeman fries up a good batch of eggs and bacon."

Fred leaned forward on the desktop looking steadily at O'Bryon. He swallowed hard several times and in the end did not speak.

Kelly arose. "I'm goin' up to the rooming house. Care to come along?"

Through clenched teeth Tower said, "Later," and after O'Bryon had departed he scowled perplexedly at the roadway door. Kelly looked as good as new and he'd drunk just as much as Fred had. Maybe Irishmen could handle whiskey after all; maybe they just naturally passed out a lot. In any case it did not matter. Fred stood up. Evidently the coffee had worked a small miracle, for although his knee hurt, the rest of him felt better than it had been an hour earlier.

He left the jailhouse heading for his harness shop. Across the road the man who clerked at the general store was sweeping off the sidewalk. He leaned on his broom watching Tower go up the opposite plankwalk and pursed his lips in disapproval.

CHAPTER 21

A
Day Later

CONSTABLE Cutler allowed himself to be shaved and washed. He did not feel especially hungry until Bertha Maloney brought an old motheaten throw rug to cover the floor-stain where Sawyer Kent had died. Even then his appetite did not improve very much.

Kelly O'Bryon came to see him. So did Jim McGregor from the bank. There would have been others but Bertha firmly turned them away in the hall. As a practical man McGregor wanted the details of what had happened last night and Walt gave them to him. McGregor sat like an oversized stuffed toy looking at his clasped hands. The only comment he made was to the effect that he just could not believe Mr. White's rangeboss would do things like that, and Kelly, who was sitting on the sill of the broken window, was irreverent enough to say from what he'd seen and heard lately, Mack Kelso was capable of doing anything.

McGregor ignored that remark and gazed at Constable Cutler. "Mr. White will be stunned. He put a lot of store by Mack."

Walt said nothing. Whether Mr. White would be stunned or not was his problem; Walt had enough problems of his own. After the banker departed, O'Bryon appropriated the chair McGregor had been sitting on and said, "That man I hit over the head was sittin' up in his cell with his head in his hands. I got to tell you that was a relief to me. I thought I'd busted his skull."

Walt said, "How is Fred?"

Kelly considered his answer carefully before offering it.

"Tired, and his knee pains him. Otherwise he'll be all right by afternoon . . . There's a lot of folks in town who can't get over what happened. I guess they needed something to talk about to replace a lot of worn-out gossip . . . What do you want done with the prisoners?"

"They got to be fed and watered," Walt answered absently. "Someone'll have to ride shotgun on them."

Kelly's eyes widened. "Why? They're locked in like animals in cages."

It was the law that prisoners had to be treated well. "Someone to fetch grub over to them from the café," he told O'Bryon. "See that they get to go across the alley to the outhouse, and so forth."

O'Bryon shrugged. "Fred and I can look after them, I guess. How long do you expect it'll be?"

"Until the circuit-rider gets to Peralta; I'd say he ought to ride in maybe in a week or ten days and set up court like he always does at the fire hall . . . And I got to get out of this bed and prepare written charges, round up witnesses, and so forth."

O'Bryon gazed at the bed. "You're not goin' to get up," he said quietly, then broke into a wide grin. "I got to tell you, Walt, you do a better job on your back at keepin' the peace than you do on your feet."

Walt let that remark pass, and after O'Bryon had departed, Bertha brought his breakfast. The hot coffee was very welcome; otherwise he ate little. The sun was climbing when Elizabeth Bartlett came in looking solemn and big-eyed. When she had shaved him earlier he had not said ten words; she had assumed that something was troubling him and had done nothing to force talk between them.

Now, he watched her cross to bedside from the doorway and smiled. "How's your elbow?" he asked, and pointed in the direction of the chair.

She sat down, looked at the broken window, and from the side of her eye glanced at the throw rug on her opposite side. "My elbow is much better, thank you.' How do you feel?"

"Fine. Stronger every day."

"I thought you might be having a relapse. When I washed and shaved you, you didn't want to talk."

"I never do before I've had coffee, Elizabeth." As he held her gaze he decided again that she was really a very handsome woman. She broke the silence by mentioning that she thought she would leave the country; go east or perhaps out to California.

Evidently Bertha had not mentioned the two of them leaving together for a while. Walt groped for his makings and used the rolling of a smoke as an excuse for his delayed response.

When he had lighted up he said, "I guess the fire wiped you out."

She nodded. "Yes. Everything. We have a pair of harness horses out there somewhere but one is lame. I don't think they'd bring much but I'd like to find them." She raised her eyes to his face. "Maybe sell them for whatever I could get."

He wanted to mention her husband's ashes but refrained. It was none of his business anyway, except that he was protective toward her. Instead he said, "I think I can get out of this bed."

She stared at him. "You can do no such a thing, Mr. Cutler. Do you want to open the wounds again?"

He ignored the question. "What's the difference between moving around in a bed or in a buggy?"

She was exasperated with him. "If you get out of that bed Bertha and I'll find a big strong man to sit in here and keep you in it. Can't you get it through your head that—?"

"Do you play checkers, Elizabeth?"

His interruption caught her in midbreath. She stared at him, then finally nodded her head and softened her tone. "Yes."

"Well, Elizabeth, not being able to get out of this confounded bed day in and day out . . ." He saw a darkness come into her eyes and could have kicked himself.

She stared at him through an interval of quiet, then arose and left the room. He looked helplessly at the closed door. Someone once told him that every living human being makes a fool of himself for at least five minutes of every day. Right now he thought that he had multiplied that by about thirty, and it wasn't even noon yet.

Then she was back in the doorway holding an old checkerboard and a cigar box with the checkers in it. She efficiently put the guns on the floor, arranged the little bedside table so that he could reach it easily, and pulled up the chair. Without a word she arranged the board and opened the cigar box, then, finally, she raised her eyes to his face and said, "Blacks or reds?"

He chose the black checkers.

Her simple answer to his query about whether she knew how to play checkers had been an understatement. She beat Walt three games straight running and as they positioned their checkers for the fourth game he eyed her a little skeptically.

"Elizabeth . . . ?"

She was arranging her checkers and did not meet his gaze. "I learned to play as a child. On rainy days at the orphanage we either played checkers or sewed. I couldn't sew." Her eyes swept up to his face, showing a very faint twinkle. "Your move, Constable Cutler."

He was not concentrating as he reached toward the board. "Yesterday it was Walt. Today it's Constable Cutler."

She did not answer. She watched his move and made one to counter it. Then she said, "You might do better if you'd moved a center piece, Walt."

He lost that game too and as she was folding the board after boxing the checkers he said, "How about mumbly peg?" and she laughed. It was the first time he'd heard her do that.

Someone entered from the porch and let the door slam. They both listened and he relaxed first. "It's Fred Tower."

He was correct; Fred limped to the doorway, eyed them both from wet dark eyes, nodded toward Elizabeth, and when she arose to depart, he said, "Ma'am, you're welcome to stay. I just came up to tell the constable Mack Kelso says you either got to make a formal charge or turn him loose."

Walt looked ruefully at the older man. "I'll make a charge as soon as I can get hold of some paper and a pencil. Anyway, I got the right to hold him for twenty-four hours on suspicion."

Fred nodded because evidently none of this seemed to bother him very much. "Jim McGregor had one of the stage drivers send a telegraph message to Mr. White from the wireless office down at Mineral Wells. The driver told me that himself."

Walt shrugged. "Suits me. I'd like Mr. White to get back here too."

Fred shifted his weight and cleared his throat. "Doc Eaton's back," he announced.

That surprised both Walt Cutler and Elizabeth Bartlett. "He just left yesterday," Walt said.

Fred nodded about that. "Yeah. Well, he's back, and he came to the jailhouse wanting to look at Sackett and the dead man."

"What did he say about them?"

"That except for Frank Sackett having a skull of solid bone Kelly would have busted it. About Kent, all he said was that he'd make out a certificate . . . I guess that means Kent is dead." Fred's lips pulled downward. "It's sure a relief to know that, ain't it? And he made a certificate for Sexton too."

Elizabeth started toward the door, Fred moved clear, and as she reached the hallway beyond, she turned and said, "Walt . . . promise me, please, that you won't get out of that bed?"

For some reason he did not understand Walt got red in the face as he promised her, then she was gone and Fred Tower was back leaning in the doorway gazing at him, this time with pursed lips and widened dark eyes.

Another visitor came in from out front and let the door slam. Fred learned back just enough to see the length of the hallway, then straightened up speaking in a loud whisper. "Speak of the devil . . ."

Dr. Eaton approached Fred with a sardonic look on his face. "You were right," he said. "I should have waited another day," then he edged past into the room, approached the side of the bed, and with a faint vertical line between his brows, studied the constable's face. "How do you feel?" he asked. Before Walt could speak Dr. Eaton flipped back the blankets and leaned down as he spoke again. "You want to know why I'm back? Well, because there's no rest for the wicked and two stage horses lamed up." Eaton shot Walt a dark look. "The driver said he could not make it all the way down to Mineral Wells with only two using horses, so he turned back . . . I understand you were busy last night, Constable. Hold still, please . . . The dressing looks very good. No leakage under there . . . As I said, you have the constitution of an ox."

Walt reached for the covers. "Good enough to go buggy riding, Doctor?"

Eaton turned in exaggerated despair toward the lanky man leaning in the doorway and made a gesture of futility. "The worst patient I ever had. He'd kill himself if I'd let him . . . How is your leg?"

Fred nodded woodenly. He did not like doctors and he particularly did not like this one. "Good enough to stand on."

"Of course it is. That's why you're not putting your weight on it."

Fred locked his jaw and pushed up off the doorjamb to stand on both legs, his expression unfriendly. He started to turn. "I'll be back later," he told Walt and went marching down the hall. Ordinarily he was not so touchy. After last night he was not up to listening to sarcasm from someone he did not care for.

Eaton already knew most of the details of the events in Walt's room last night. But there was one thing no one had been able to tell him because O'Bryon was not at the jailhouse when he walked in, and Fred was not communicative today.

"Who tried to brain that cowboy named Sackett?"

Walt jutted his jaw in the direction of the window. "He went out through there like a big bird and someone in the dark hit him over the head with a gun barrel. Why. How bad is it?"

"Not too bad, but it would have been if he'd had a thinner skull . . . Constable, I think you are one of those individuals toward whom violence and trouble naturally gravitates."

Having got that off his chest Dr. Eaton left the room, and as Walt listened to his diminishing footsteps, he wondered if the people down at Mineral Wells found Ned Eaton as objectionable as he did. Probably not. He'd been practicing medicine down there for a number of years.

Bertha brought a thick crockery bowl full of hot stew. She put it on the little bedside table and straightened back, both hands on her hips, looking at Walt Cutler with the steely gaze he was familiar with. "I understand you want to go buggy riding," she said.

Walt blinked at her.

"Don't give me that look, Walt Cutler. I was a married woman for a long time. Even if you could stand riding in a buggy you'd ought to have the decency to allow Elizabeth Bartlett a few months for her grieving."

He stared. He had not asked Elizabeth to go buggy riding, he had simply asked her what the difference was between lying in bed and sitting up in a buggy. "Is that what she told you?" he asked, and Bertha's stare did not soften when she replied.

"I didn't hear all she was telling me because I was boiling the laundry out back when she came along to help, but I heard the buggy riding part, and, Constable Cutler, I didn't come down in the last rain."

He expelled a long breath. People who misunderstood, and had feisty dispositions, too, were everywhere. This one in particular might have annoyed him if he did not feel so heavily obligated to her. He could not think of a good retort so contented himself by sounding contrite as he said, "You're right. I'll give her time for grieving."

Immediately the iron went out of Bertha Maloney's eyes and heart. She leaned to pat his hand as she softly said, "Be patient, Constable. Women aren't like horses." She patted him again and left the room.

He did not know what she had meant by comparing women to horses, and he turned toward the bowl of aromatic stew like a starving man. Now, at last, he was hungry. About the rest of the recent interlude in his room with Bertha Maloney, he was willing to forget it entirely.

She probably was too, because when she returned to the backyard where the laundry cauldrons were simmering she told

Elizabeth that the constable would not press her any more to go buggy riding with him until she was through her mourning period, and Elizabeth stared at Bertha's bent back at the big iron pots with the same expression of astonishment and bafflement Walt Cutler had shown a short while earlier.

A little later when Bertha paused to wipe perspiration from her brow she fished an envelope from her apron pocket and considered it with a scowl. "Dr. Eaton handed me this." She held it up for Elizabeth's inspection. "No name on it. He handed it to me as he was leaving a while back and told me to open it one week from today." She stuffed the envelope back into her apron pocket, sighed, and turned back to the laundry pots as she said, "Probably a bill; the way they charge nowadays they want to be a long way off before folks see what they charge."

CHAPTER 22

"Open That Door!"

THREE days after the gunfire at the rooming house Peralta was back to near-normal. The Horseshoe remained the meeting ground for men who chose to dissect the recent trouble as though they had nothing else to fill their lives, which patently some did not have.

Dr. Eaton paid a final trip to Walt's room, then drove south in his own, repaired buggy leaving two certificates of death on the desk at the jailhouse for Fred and Kelly to ignore.

Mack Kelso and his riders were sullenly angry. Even after Kelly waved the handwritten complaint against them from the far side of the cell bars, they still demanded to be freed.

Elizabeth finally lost a game of checkers to Walt Cutler. That was shortly after she had shaved and washed him on the third day. He was as surprised as she was when he beat her but had enough presence of mind not to show it, and immediately challenged her to another game. Afterwards he reiterated what people had probably been saying since the Year One: Quit while you are ahead. She beat him handily, then ameliorated the annoyance by disappearing for an hour and returning holding a freshly baked cake on a thick white dish. As she cut him a wedge large enough to choke a cow she smiled and said, "Mr. Heinz rode into town a while back."

He accepted this scrap of information without allowing the fork on its way to his mouth to even falter, acknowledging her announcement by bobbing his head. The cake was still hot from the oven. As he gorged he tried to remember the last time he'd had cake straight from the oven and failed.

She watched him with interest. When he held forth the plate

for his third wedge she simply took the plate and fork from him, and made a statement that stopped his protest before it was fully out.

"I got a buggy yesterday from Mr. O'Bryon and went out to the neck."

He studied her face and waited for the rest of it.

"There . . . was nothing left. Not even the woodshed."

"Your horses?"

"I saw them in the distance but didn't try to catch them." She looked at the hands in her lap. "A wise woman told me that for every ending there is a fresh beginning." She raised her face. "There was nothing to bury, Walt. Nothing to bring back with me but pain and ache."

He said, "And memories."

She nodded at him. "Yes. Memories."

"The wise woman—was her name Bertha Maloney?"

"Yes. We share something, but with her it was quick and numbing. With me, it took a terrible year, and pain, and crying, and being heartsick from the time I awakened until I watched the moon rise. When he died it wasn't the same man . . . I stood out there waiting for a warm, soft breeze to touch my face, or maybe some wildflowers to nod, or even for the clouds to form something . . . There was nothing."

He could see the pain and dryness in her eyes and sought desperately for something to say that would help. On an inspiration he offered a simple sentence. "Love don't die, Elizabeth, it takes new forms and different directions but it lasts forever. As long as we last. From one person to another."

She jumped up and ran out of the room.

He sat propped against the pillow feeling suddenly more exhausted than if he'd run a mile. He looked at what remained of the cake she had baked him. It was very difficult to think, to order a sequence of rational thoughts. He lay back and closed his eyes.

It was sundown when Kelly O'Bryon came to say they'd have to bury Sexton and Sawyer Kent. Walt nodded. He felt neither one thing nor another for the man he had killed, any

more than he had felt for his partner Ron Sexton whom
Elizabeth had killed.

Kelly eyed him worriedly. "You look poorly. Worse than
you've looked since we brought you in here. Is the wound
botherin' you? I could get old Bellingham or the midwife to
come have a look at you."

Walt pushed up a small smile. "I'm all right."

Kelly pointed. "Did you eat all that cake?"

"Yeah."

"No wonder you look peaked. A man in your condition
hadn't ought to eat anything but rare meat and potatoes; builds
up the blood."

"I'm tired is all, Kelly. Go ahead and bury those two.
Someday I'll look them up in the dodgers."

"Missus Bartlett got a rig from me yesterday and drove out to
the neck."

"Yeah, I know. She told me. There wasn't anything to bury
. . . Kelly, she's got a team out there, one's lame, the other's a
little long in the teeth. She wants to sell them. If you had the
time you could ride out, catch 'em, and bring them back to
town."

O'Bryon puffed out his cheeks. "I know the pair. I saw 'em
from a distance." He eyed Walt. "You know what they're
worth. I don't want to offer her that. She don't have anything,
being burned out and all."

"Give her a hundred dollars for them, Kelly."

O'Bryon jumped and his eyes popped wide open.

"And I'll give you the hundred and you can keep the horses."

Kelly recovered slowly. "Oh. Well, I guess like that I can do
it. Walt, they're not worth thirty dollars for the pair of 'em."

"Yeah."

"All right. I'll go out in the morning." Kelly removed his hat
and inspected the inside sweatband. "Jim McGregor says the
town council don't like having to foot the bill for Kelso and his
crew. They got quite a bill run up at the café."

Anger stirred in the constable. "Maybe we'd ought to turn
them loose," he said. "They'll need a grubstake to start over

with somewhere else; they could rob the bank. Who would stop them?"

Kelly pulled at his hat brim, looking toward the door. "I'll have to hire a couple of grave diggers tomorrow to dig those graves. Jim'll have a fit about that too, I expect."

"If he says anything hand him the shovel."

O'Bryon departed looking preoccupied. When he reached the jailhouse where Fred had just finished feeding the prisoners Kelly related what Walt had told him about the horses out at the stump ranch and Fred showed no surprise. He rattled the coffeepot atop the stove, swore because it was empty, and went to a chair to sit down. His knee was much better, nearly all the swelling was gone, but from habit he still favored it. As he sat down he put a squinty gaze upon the liveryman. "You notice anything odd up there?"

Kelly frowned. "At the rooming house?"

"Yes."

"Odd? No, I can't say as I did."

Fred snorted. "Then you're not lookin' at things right. Would you give that lady a hundred dollars for her old horses, one lamed up?"

Kelly did not reply. He would not have answered that question up at the rooming house so he would not answer it at the jailhouse, but Fred persevered. "Well, would you have?"

O'Bryon's temper flared. "What are you gettin' at?"

"You wouldn't and neither would I and neither would anyone else in their right mind, unless they . . . Haven't you noticed how he looks at her?"

Kelly had noticed nothing. He sank down upon a wall bench looking across the room. For a long while he was silent, then he said, "Well, what's wrong with that? She's as pretty as a speckled bird. And she sure don't back up, her and that scattergun." The longer Kelly talked the better he sounded to himself, and he admired Elizabeth Bartlett. "Fred, you remember last month at a poker session in the Horsehoe card room we got to teasin' you about her?"

Fred remembered very well but he was not going to

acknowledge that he remembered so he simply sat there and waited for the rest of it.

"You should have rode out there," Kelly stated with an incredible lack of tact. "You'd have maybe got the inside track. I'll tell you straight out, countin' me there's likely fifty, sixty men right here in Peralta who'd spark her in a minute if they thought they stood a chance . . . I think you're one of them but you won't admit it."

Fred Tower was red in the face. For a moment an old friendship teetered upon the verge of violent dissolution, then Kelly smiled and said, "I think you'd stand a better chance than the rest of them. You got a nice appearance and two good businesses, the tannery and the harness works."

Fred's shoulders gradually loosened and the color slowly left his face. He said, "You got a chew?"

Kelly tossed over his plug and when he got it back he bit off a corner; they sat in the gathering late-day shadows looking at one another until Fred heaved up to his feet and went to open the door and glance up and down the roadway for no reason except that he felt an urge to breathe fresh air.

There were six horsemen reining to a halt at the rack thirty feet away. He recognized the Heinzes and their hired riders and started to call a friendly greeting, but old Gus turned, looked Fred directly in the eye and said, "You still got Mack and them other bastards in there, Fred?"

Gus's sons and his riders were un-shipping carbines from saddle boots. Fred stopped chewing; he almost stopped breathing. There was a stranger with them—which Fred might have missed noticing except that he did not dismount, and now he sat up there like a big bump on a log, and when Fred stared at him, the stranger looked like he'd been yanked through a knothole; someone had beat the hell out of him.

Gus took down his lariat and glared. "I asked you a question!"

Fred's grip on the edge of the door tightened. "Yeah, they're in here. Why?"

Gus started toward the plankwalk and Fred slammed the

door, barred it, and turned so fast he almost fell when his injured knee reacted to the abrupt twist. He yelled at O'Bryon. "It's the Heinzes!"

Kelly sprang to his feet. It took no more than a second to read the expression on Tower's face. Kelly turned toward the wall-rack where three saddleguns, two shotguns, and a long-barreled Remington rifle were loosely chained.

A pistol butt struck the roadway door and Gus snarled a demand for them to un-bar the door.

Fred watched O'Bryon grab the chain and pull it through trigger-guards. He yelled back. "I'm not goin' to open the door. What's wrong with you, Gus?"

The next time the door shook it was from the steel butt-plate of a carbine. "You open it, Fred, or we'll blow it off its hinges!"

Kelly checked the barrels of one of the shotguns and tossed it to Fred Tower. He then checked the loads of the second shotgun and caught the sight of movement at one of the little barred front-wall windows as he was snapping the shotgun back into firing position. He raised the gun and fired. The sound nearly deafened the men in the little office, glass blew outwards, and someone jumping backwards fell heavily to the plankwalk, and through the diminishing echoes of the gun-blast a shrill voice yelled curses.

Fred yelled back. "Gus, get away from here. All of you get away from here. The next shot'll take somebody's head off . . . What is wrong with you?"

For a long moment there was silence. Then a carbine made its flat, sharp sound and a slug came through the door, struck the little wood-stove, and flattened there.

Gus Heinz's voice when he spoke again was thick with fury. "You open that door or we'll blow it off and hang you right alongside those other cattle stealin' sons of bitches. You hear me, Fred?"

Fred looked back at O'Bryon, his face twisted into an expression of angry bafflement. "Three days later he comes back like this because Kelso's crew stole cattle?"

Kelly made a wild guess. "They been drinkin'."

But Fred did not think so. He had known Gus Heinz a long time; he was not a drinking man. A drink now and then but never more than two.

"It's more'n that. He's not drunk, Kelly, I stood out there lookin' at him. He's mad—mad all the way through." Fred raised his voice again. "Gus, what is this all about?"

"Open that door and you'll find out," Heinz bawled back, and someone fired another round through the door, this time making Fred Tower wince then duck low to get beneath the broken window and to the farther north corner of the room.

Fred spat out his cud and hunkered down holding the shotgun like a staff in front. Kelly was down near the back of the room watching both windows but no one attempted to peek in again. Kelly sounded like a man making a mild protest when he said, "Right here in the middle of town for Chrissake, with it still bein' daylight." With the time finally to recover from astonishment, he looked at Tower wearing an expression of disbelief. "He can't get away with this. It's crazy."

Two carbine shots slammed into the door this time, but in the direction of the hinges. One struck wood but the other bullet hit steel and made an unnerving sound as it ricocheted.

There was nothing more for Fred and Kelly to say to one another. Crazy or not Gus Heinz was going to shoot his way into the jailhouse if he possibly could, and if in the process its two defenders stopped bullets, Gus would probably regret that later because basically he was a man with a conscience, but that would be after he'd taken the prisoners out and lynched them, and by then neither Kelly nor Fred would know anything about that.

They could not reason with Gus; he was unreasoningly angry. Neither Kelly nor Fred had ever seen him like this before. But Fred wanted to make one final effort so he yelled out:

"Hey, Gus, what you got against Kelly and me? We're the only ones in here."

"No, you're not," the cowman bellowed in reply. "I got

nothin' against either of you, but if you try to stop us from gettin' at Kelso and his thievin' riders . . .''

This time when someone fired from outside it was with a handgun. The large slug struck the latch and demolished it, but the door was barred from the inside.

CHAPTER 23

A Legend
for Peralta

WHEN the gunfire erupted a dozen men lounging along the bar at the Horseshoe rushed to the front windows to look across the road southward, but none of them made any attempt to use the doorway to go outside where visibility would have been better, and at the general store, which was on the same side of the road as the saloon but farther southward, the proprietor was startled, but his clerk, who had already demonstrated his dread of violence when Tower and Sackett had tangled, almost jumped out of his skin.

They had been in the act of putting the day's receipts in the safe before closing up for the day. It was suppertime, there had been no customers for the last half hour, and normally this was the period when they could relax.

Elsewhere around Peralta, even among the people who had seen Gus Heinz leading his riders into town, every one of them armed to the teeth, there was a period of wild confusion after the gunfire erupted. There had been very few people abroad before, but afterwards Main Street did not have a soul in sight for its full length.

At the rooming house where Bertha and Elizabeth were resting in the kitchen after doing the laundry, and where Walt Cutler was dozing while late-day shadows stole into his room through the broken window, the abrupt, unexpected thunder of gunfire brought him upright in the bed with a pounding heart.

Someone rushed in from the roadway allowing the door to slam as they hastened down the hallway. Walt heard Bertha intercept whoever it was with a challenge, and recognized the answering voice. It was Jim McGregor, who never seemed to get excited, but he was excited now as he replied to Bertha. "Heinz . . . He's down at the jailhouse attacking the place with his boys and his hired riders."

Moments later the heavyset banker burst into Walt's room, his expression not much different from most other expressions around town; he was astounded, simply incredulous. Without bothering to close the door he said, "Walt! Gus with his whole crew is attacking the jailhouse! I couldn't believe it." McGregor stood wide-legged, a large, thick man whose face showed a degree of astonishment he probably had not shown in years. "Shooting through the door!" McGregor gestured wildly. "Gus and his sons and their three hired riders . . . He's acting like a madman."

Bertha, who had been hovering just beyond in the hallway, turned briskly away in the direction of the roadside door. McGregor fished out a white handkerchief and mopped at his face. Walt said, "Is there someone inside, Jim?" He knew the answer in his heart before McGregor replied. "Someone said Fred and Kelly are in there but I don't really know . . . I do know there's someone in there with a shotgun because when I looked out the bank window a shotgun blast blew out one of the jailhouse front windows from inside."

McGregor tucked his handkerchief in a pocket and got better control of himself. He looked at the man in the bed as his excitement diminished, then he made a loud rattling sigh and shook his head. "Gus must be crazy. Stockmen can't just ride into a town and start shooting up the jailhouse . . . He's got someone with him, a stranger as near as I could tell from up at the bank." McGregor flapped his arms, indicating his disbelief that this was happening and his helpless feeling about it.

Bertha came to the doorway to ignore Jim McGregor and look directly at Walt as she spoke. "There are six of them. I watched one of them leading their horses away. They have a man with them I never saw before, but it's getting along toward the time of day when it's hard to see from up here down there . . . But I know Mr. Heinz, and I know his boys from seeing them around town . . . Constable, they're going to break into the jailhouse. There's not another human being in sight."

Walt heard the gunfire increase. He also heard two shotguns roar and could guess who was inside firing them. McGregor and Bertha Maloney were looking steadily at him. He waited for a lull in the firing, then asked Bertha where his britches were, and surprisingly, she turned to walk briskly away without a single word of argument.

But Jim McGregor's gaze clouded with doubts. "You can't go down there," he said, adding an additional sentence which was lost when the gunfire was resumed near the center of town.

When Bertha returned, Elizabeth was with her, eyes very dark, features distraught, but she said nothing as Bertha put Walt's trousers, shirt, and hat on the bed, and placed his boots on the floor nearby.

Bertha straightened up. All three of them stared toward the bed. McGregor finally wagged his head as he fished for his white handkerchief again. "You can't do it. You'll kill yourself. I'll try and get some men from around town." He was facing the open door when Walt stopped him.

"You get a posse, Jim, and in the mood I think Gus is in, you're going to be up to your gullet in a battle."

McGregor made that flapping gesture of helplessness again. "If McGregor gets inside the jailhouse, Walt, there are goin' to be dead men anyway. The crazy fool, what's he after?"

"He's after Kelso and the men who ride with him, and I think I know why. If I'm right Gus is goin' to take them out and hang them . . . Elizabeth, help me, will you?"

She approached the bed with a white face. Instead of helping him as he threw back the covers, she placed a hand against his chest to prevent him from turning to sit upon the edge of the bed. "You can't do it," she said so softly only he heard the words. "Walt, you're healing wonderfully . . . You'll tear everything loose and bleed to death—for what?"

He met her darkened gaze, offered no answer to her question, and started to maneuver his body gently to the edge of the bed. He was encouraged because as he did this there was no pain. He sat a moment listening to the gunfire, then resolutely reached for his trousers. The room dimmed, his mind seemed to be losing the ability to sponsor thought, and dizziness would have let him fall except for Elizabeth. She caught him. Under McGregor's stare the women got him back into bed and covered. Then Bertha turned in anger upon the banker. "What do you expect a lawman in Peralta to do to earn his thirty dollars a month—kill himself?"

McGregor met Bertha's anger in silence and gazed at the man in the bed. He was a banker, had been nothing else for most of his life, and what little trouble had come into his life since early manhood had not involved guns. But many years ago, Jim McGregor had been familiar with guns and trouble. He turned toward the door and Bertha spoke to him again, in a less hostile but equally brittle a tone of voice. "Find some men and bring them back here." At McGregor's puzzled frown she explained. "All right, Walt wants to go down and put a stop to this. You want the same thing. Find some strong men and bring them back here . . . He'll be ready, Mr. McGregor."

The banker stared at her, drifted a questioning gaze toward the bed, then back to Bertha, and finally he walked out into the hall. He understood what she had not mentioned.

The moment he was gone Bertha came to bedside and glowered. She picked up the shirt and leaned forward. "Hold your arm out. Good. Now sit up and hold the other one out . . . Elizabeth, fold the blankets back. Constable, don't lift your legs, we'll scoot the pants on you without that. Just—that's the idea, just keep your legs straight out . . . Now then, this part is going to hurt, I expect; Elizabeth, get an arm under him. Good. Constable, your pants are on. You can button them."

Bertha stepped back to examine what had been accomplished. She shook her head but said nothing until she had his boots in her hand. Then she handed one to Elizabeth with instructions. "Gently. Don't yank on them."

When they were finished Bertha went in search of Constable Cutler's hat, and during her absence, the two remaining people in the room looked at one another. Walt had sweat on his upper lip; getting the trousers into place had been painful but now there was no pain. He pointed to the unloaded shotgun. "Please . . . ?"

She handed it to him. He looked around for the one good load, found it, and dropped it into one side of the gun and asked if she could find a few more loads. She stood firm. He cocked an eye at her. "Elizabeth, I need your help."

A sudden scald of tears impaired her sight. She ran out of the room and nearly collided with Bertha. She said, "He wants shells for your shotgun," in a voice of desperation and Bertha matter-of-factly told her where to find them, then went back into the room with Walt's hat. She dropped it atop his head and looked him over before saying, "You look like a scarecrow. Suppose Mr. McGregor can't find stretcher-bearers?"

Walt was eyeing that pony bottle of untouched whiskey Fred had brought him in what now seemed like ages ago. "Why then I expect I'll have to crawl down there on my hands and knees, won't I?" he replied.

Bertha's tough mouth loosened slightly. "And I thought my husband was pig-headed. Constable, what do you think you can accomplish?"

He looked at her when he replied. "I don't know. How many times in your life have you had to do something you figured might fail but you had to try anyway, Bertha?"

She turned that over in her mind, then changed the subject by pointing to the pony of whiskey. "A couple of swallows of that might help."

Elizabeth turned with a handful of shotgun shells and stood watching Walt load the empty side. About the time their eyes met, loud-talking men let the roadway door slam after entering the parlor on their way down the hall.

Jim McGregor was in the lead, without his coat or tie, which was unusual for the banker. Two of the men with him worked at the blacksmith shop and knew both Bertha and Constable Cutler. The third man was shorter than the other three, with a head and neck the same size and a torso of pure brawn. He

was one of the hostlers from the corralyard, and grinned at
Constable Cutler.

McGregor was in charge. When he had everyone in place he
eyed the door opening and said, "All right, lift. You better hang
on, Walt, we got to tip the bed to get it through the doorway."

They were four strong men. Even the banker, who was
paunchy now and soft, was basically a very strong man. It
helped too that with two on each side of the bed, the load was
well distributed and easy to handle. What might have been too
much for two men was easily manageable by four men.

No one realized there was silence near the center of town
where before there had been gunfire because they had to
concentrate on getting Walt on his bed through the doorway,
then down the hall toward the roadway beyond.

Elizabeth, who went ahead to hold the porch door open, said,
"There's no one down there. The road is empty."

She was correct, there was no one in sight upon either side of
the road, but there was oily smoke like a lingering pale fog in the
roadway where the attackers had been.

Once clear of the second door McGregor signaled his
helpers to lower the bed, then everyone stood in silence trying to
guess where the stockmen were who had been attacking the
jailhouse. Walt had the shotgun beside his right leg with his
hand on it. The longer they remained motionless the more he
began to suspect that the worst had happened, that Gus Heinz
had shot his way into the jailhouse.

McGregor turned with a puzzled frown to look down at the
constable, a question in his eyes. Walt had no answer; he had no
idea why the fight had stopped or where the attackers were.
What he did know was that Gus Heinz had not given up, even if
he were inside the jailhouse. He said, "You boys ready?" and as
they lifted him on the bed he raised the shotgun so he could hold
it with both hands.

When they were as far as the harness works Fred Tower's
hired man stepped gingerly into the recessed doorway and
craned around to see who was making sounds like marching
men. When he saw the bed coming and Walt Cutler on it

holding a shotgun, Jake's mouth dropped open. He did not recover from surprise until the bed-carriers were almost to the doorway, then he faded back inside and remained motionless in shadows until the strange cavalcade had passed by.

McGregor called for another halt midway between the harness works and the jailhouse. He was sweating like a bull in a harem of heifers and had to use his white handkerchief again.

There was not a sound across the road or down at the jailhouse. There should have been some noise; if Heinz was inside the jailhouse there should have been a lot of noise. McGregor turned his craggy face toward Walt. "What do you make of it? Should we go on down there?"

Walt knew all five men were waiting for his words. He did not know that there were two women ten feet behind him and could not have turned around to look at them if he had known.

"The jailhouse," he said quietly, and added a short sentence that unsettled his sweating companions. "There are men over yonder in the general store."

For a moment the bed-carriers looked in the direction of the general store. It had probably occurred to them that if they attempted to carry the constable inside the jailhouse, and if those men over at the emporium were the Heinzes and their riders, they might start firing again. The short, massive man was squinting across the road when he said, "Mr. Cutler, do you expect it might do any good if one of us went over and palavered with those gents in the store?"

A lanky man with a prominent Adam's apple, who worked at the blacksmith shop, was looking back. He spoke in a slow drawl when he said, "Ain't no need, gents. Look yonder. It's them ladies. They're already near the plankwalk over yonder."

Walt forgot to move slowly; he grabbed the edge of the bed and twisted half around. The pain came immediately but he ignored it. He and his companions were like statues watching the progress of Bertha Maloney and Elizabeth Bartlett.

When the women stepped up onto the far sidewalk, Bertha's jaw was firmly set and her eyes were rummaging the area down in front of the general store, but as Elizabeth kept pace with the older woman, she turned, saw the men staring, and raised her right hand so they could see that her fingers were crossed. Walt did not appreciate that gesture and neither did James McGregor, but the other men did, and they smiled back at Elizabeth.

CHAPTER 24

End of the Trail

IT wasn't Gus Heinz who had caught shotgun pellets in the side; it was his eldest son Carl. His father and brother were working over him in grim and angry silence. The others were watching, carbines draped from their arms, and both the storekeeper and his flighty clerk were in the background looking more indignant than worried. When Bertha and Elizabeth walked in, the watchers turned to stare, less surprised at their arrival than agitated by it.

Old Gus did not even raise his head from the bloody work of picking out lead pellets until Bertha spoke from slightly to his left and behind him.

"Did you wash your hands, Mr. Heinz?"

He acted as though he had not heard her for a moment, then leaned back to look around. Bertha ignored Gus and spoke to the storekeeper. "Mr. Evans; we'll need clean hot water, a bottle of carbolic acid, some soap and clean rags." When none of the men moved, simply stood looking owlishly at her, Bertha's brows dropped a notch. "Now, Mr. Evans—if you please!" The clerk tugged at his employer's sleeve, pulling him around.

Elizabeth elbowed Gus's younger son and moved into his place as she studied the shirtless man lying on a blanket someone had spread on the floor. He had not been washed, there was blood on his torso and the blanket. She knelt, met his glassy look of pain and shock, and raised her eyes to his father's face. Old Gus's hands were bloody to the wrist; he was holding a wicked-bladed clasp knife, the tool he had been prying pellets out with. Elizabeth sounded like Bertha Maloney when she said, "You're not butchering a beef, Mr. Heinz," and Gus reddened.

As the basin of water and carbolic acid arrived Bertha shouldered Gus out of the way, hitched at her skirt, and also knelt beside the injured man. Between them the women washed Carl Heinz. That made it easier to locate the little punctures. Bertha leaned down, made her examination, and said, "Mr. Evans—some tweezers and gauze."

There was not a sound as the women went to work. Fortunately for Carl Heinz he had not caught the full charge, and what had hit him had done so as the blast blew past him. Nevertheless they had dropped six little pellets into the plate the store clerk had provided before he groaned and attempted to raise his head and turn it. Elizabeth said, "Stop moving." Carl obeyed. Bertha probed for the one deep pellet, heard her patient grinding his teeth, and without a shred of mercy said, "What did you expect; who do you think you are; you acted like a band of renegade In'ians . . . Stop fidgeting!"

Carl Heinz gasped. "Whiskey!"

When the men began to get un-tracked she flashed a cold look around at them. "No whiskey!" They stopped moving and she went back to work. As she dropped the deepest pellet into the dish and reared back on her haunches to dip her hands in the basin and dry them she sought old Gus's face. "For your sake I hope the men inside the jailhouse aren't drunk. Constable Cutler's over there with some townsmen."

Gus lifted his head and squinted past the doorway. It was not possible that Walt would be across the road. Gus saw them, saw the bed and the man on it holding a shotgun, and walked as far as the doorway as though he needed verification of what his eyes told him.

Walt waited until someone emerged from the store, then recognized Heinz, and without having to raise his voice, said, "Gus, you're under arrest."

Heinz continued to stand in the shaded doorway, squinting for a while, then he leaned his Winchester aside and started across the road. Jim McGregor and the other man standing around the bed watched Gus from closed, hostile faces. When Heinz stepped up onto the plankwalk he ignored everyone but Constable Cutler. "I got a little surprise for you," he said bleakly. "It wasn't just White's cattle Mack was rustling . . . My crew and I went north a few days back to look for our calvy heifers." Gus paused for effect. "There was the sign as plain as the nose on your face; someone had been stealing our cattle. Not just three or four head like settlers do, bands of them, and they pushed them into a bigger herd and taken 'em over the hills where they met some buyers and sold 'em. We tracked the last drive, Walt. Took two days." Gus paused again, and this time thrust his face closer as he said, "An' we met a man over yonder who was part of a band who'd been buyin' those stolen cattle." Gus's look of triumph was tinged with bitterness. "We brought him back with us. He's over yonder in the store with his ankles and hands tied. Him and us came to an understanding after some consideration. His name is Amos Peters—that's what he told us, and it don't matter anyway. He told us as near as he recalled they'd brought about two hunnert head of Heinz critters along with five times that many with White's brand on 'em . . . Walt, you still think I shouldn't have come down here to get Kelso and his dirty thievin' friends?" Gus straightened up wearing an expression of bleak triumph. "Folks have been hanging cattle thieves as far back as I can remember. That's been range law since—"

"Range law your butt," Walt said sharply. "I'm not going to bother to tell you how many laws you broke since you rode into town today and tried to kill Fred Tower and Kelly O'Bryon and take my prisoners out of the jailhouse. I'm going to lock you up, Gus, and if you start another fight I'm goin' to call in the army . . . Who got hurt?"

Heinz stood stiffly outraged, small blue eyes fixed upon the constable. Down at the jailhouse someone raised a rough voice in a shout. "Hey, you want some more?"

No one reacted until Walt spoke to the banker. "Someone ought to go down and see if they got hurt in there." McGregor took the lanky blacksmith's helper with him. When Fred and

Kelly opened the door they nodded toward McGregor but kept a wary watch on the front of the general store. They refused to leave the jailhouse or put down their weapons until they heard Walt tell Gus Heinz to yell across the road for his riders not to shoot.

When McGregor returned with Kelly and Fred they looked stonily at Gus Heinz; there was plenty of fight left in both of them. Walt said, "You look like hell" to Fred Tower, and for a moment he simply gazed at the constable, then laughed. "You're one to talk. Why don't you get wheels on that bed?"

Gus Heinz was staring at the storefront beyond, his face set in rigid lines. Now that it was over his thoughts were going back over what had happened when he'd entered town in a towering rage, and since then. He did not look appeased but neither did he look comfortable. Kelly O'Bryon broke the moment of awkward silence among them. "Gus, how's your boy?"

Heinz refused to look at the liveryman when he stiffly replied. "Missus Malone and that settler-lady are patchin' him up. He'll be all right." Heinz then stiffly turned his head toward the men he had tried to dislodge from the jailhouse and in a bitter voice asked a question. "How's that thievin' scum you got in the cells?"

Kelly, unlike Fred Tower, did not carry grudges or stay angry long. "Scairt pea green" he replied, studying Heinz's bleak features. "Me too, for a while."

Fred Tower did not like the way this conversation was going; he spoke coldly to Walt. "Want us to round them up and put them in the cells?"

Across the road Bertha Maloney and Elizabeth emerged from the store. Two of Heinz's riders walked as far as the door with them, smiling and friendly. Words were said which were indistinguishable to the watching men across the road, then the women started on a diagonal course toward Constable Cutler and the men with him.

Fred was unrelenting. "Walt? There's two empty cells." Townspeople appeared cautiously here and there the length of Main Street. Jim McGregor shifted to a relaxed stance, eyeing

the general store where armed men were hovering near the
doorway looking across the road.

"*Walt!*"

Cutler looked up at Tower, then at Gus Heinz. "Naw, Fred,
not now. Gus? When the damages are totaled up you can pay
them or go to jail."

Heinz refused to look around as the women stepped up
nearby on the plankwalk. He regarded Constable Cutler.
"Well . . ."

"Get your horses and leave town, Gus. Not up Main Street,
around on the east side by the alley." Walt returned Heinz's
bitter stare. "Come back by yourself in a few days. I'll have the
damages toted up by then . . . Leave that man you said bought
the stolen cattle." Walt gently wagged his head. "Range law
went out with the buffalo. Go on . . . get your riders and get out
of town."

Not a word was said until Gus was approaching the far
plankwalk, then Fred Tower, who was watching Heinz,
growled at Walt. "He tried to kill us, the old bastard. And look
at your jailhouse; it's like a million termites been eatin' away at
the front of it."

Walt too watched Heinz go across the road. Without raising
his voice he answered Fred Tower. "Range law, Fred. You
grew up with it the same as he did. It don't apply any more but
while it lasted the country grew. Without it I doubt that it
would have. He'll pay the damages . . . Fred, Gus is a good
man and you know it." When Tower faced back around, Walt
smiled at him. "I'm hungry as a wolf, how about you and
Kelly?"

Tower came down from his fierce mood a little at a time. He
and Kelly lent a hand at carrying Walt back to the rooming
house. When the bed was back in his room, McGregor and the
man he'd dragooned left the rooming house, bound unerringly
for the Horseshoe, where about half Peralta's male population
had congregated to await the arrival of someone who knew
more than they did.

Kelly O'Bryon was also bone-dry but he put off heading for

the saloon until he and Fred had given Walt the details of the attack and how they had resisted. What neither of them knew, because of smoke and excitement, was which one of them had caught Carl Heinz in the side with a wild shotgun blast. When Kelly finally departed he intended to find the outlaw cattle-buyer calling himself Amos Peters and lock him up in one of the jailhouse cells where he and the men he had bought stolen cattle from could lament in unison.

Fred Tower's indignation passed slowly, leaving him more exhausted than angry. He looked from Walt to Bertha and Elizabeth, and wagged his head. There was nothing more to be said, not today anyway. Perhaps in a month or two it would be easier to discuss all the things that had happened, but as he was preparing to leave the room he put a skeptical gaze on the man in the bed. "Knowin' you hasn't always been a pleasure," he said solemnly, "and one other thing—damned if I'm goin' to set at the same poker table with Gus Heinz come Thursday night!"

After Walt and the two women were alone in the room Bertha went to the chair and dropped down on it as though her legs could hold her up no longer. She brushed back a heavy lock of graying hair and said, "If someone had told me anything like this could happen in Peralta I wouldn't have believed them . . . How do you feel, Constable?"

He had been listening to Bertha but looking at Elizabeth. She had an uncanny knack for appearing serene when no one else could have. He was thinking this must be because she'd had to act that way throughout a life which had never treated her very well.

"Mr. Cutler! I asked how you felt!"

Walt turned his head. "Fine, Bertha. Well enough to go buggy riding."

"What about all those men in your jailhouse?"

"That'll be up to the circuit-riding judge when he gets here."

Bertha sighed, thought a moment, then leaned to rise as she said, "I want to tell you something: I think you did exactly right with Mr. Heinz. He's not a bad man. He got where he is by obeying his kind of law when there was no other kind."

Walt said nothing. He wasn't through with Gus yet; he intended to peel some hide off Gus the next time they met and sat down to talk. But he privately agreed with his landlady.

She reached the door then stopped, turned, fished in her apron, and brought forth a bedraggled envelope which she regarded with a faint frown before walking back and putting it on the bed. "You can have this," She told Walt. "Dr. Eaton left it with me with orders not to open it for a few days. I think it's his bill and he wanted to be a long way off before anyone read it."

Walt opened the envelope, extracted a single sheet of paper with one paragraph of handwriting on it. He read, sat up a little straighter and reread the paragraph, lowered his hands, and looked at Elizabeth. Both women sensed something and stood like stones.

Walt said, "It's about Sexton, Elizabeth."

Her face paled and her gray-green eyes widened.

"The rock didn't kill him," Walt said, offering Elizabeth the note. "When he fell after the rock hit him he landed atop a long sliver of hardwood sticking up out of the ground. That blood on his forehead wasn't from the rock, it was where the sliver of wood went through his head and killed him."

For five seconds no one moved or spoke, then Bertha turned a puzzled look toward Elizabeth. "What rock?" she asked. "What sliver?"

Elizabeth appeared not to have heard. She reached slowly for the note and read it twice, then raised her eyes toward the man in the bed; they were misty.

Bertha looked from one of them to the other. "What rock?" she asked again, sounding a little exasperated at being ignored. "What sliver?"

Elizabeth went over to the bed, leaned and kissed Walt on the cheek, then straightened around reaching for Bertha's arm and led the older woman out of the room and down the hall in the direction of the kitchen.

Walt listened to their retreating footfalls. Why had she kissed him, it was Ned Eaton she should have kissed. There were deepening shadows beyond the broken window. He looked out there trying to concentrate on all the loose ends he would have to satisfactorily conclude before he could put this mess behind him.

Down at the Horseshoe, Jim McGregor, Kelly, and Fred were well on the way to getting oiled. They had not paid for a single drink since entering the saloon and the longer they talked the drier they seemed to be getting.

At the jailhouse the incarcerated man who called himself Amos Peters was angry at Mack Kelso. It did not make matters any better when he said he would tell the court the absolute truth about Kelso's rustling operation, because he thought he might get clemency by doing that.

Mack said he would kill Peters. The man Heinz had captured looked through two sets of steel bars across the cell-room corridor, and wolfishly smiled. "By the time you boys get out of prison," he said, "you'll be too old to even aim a gun."

In a distant meadow with hills on three sides and nothing but ash and warped metal from a broken stove and a brass bed to indicate there had been a log house out there, a soft little breeze came from nowhere to make grass-heads bow, then it went westward and did not ever return.